MASTER OF GAMES

SIENNA SNOW

GODS OF VEGAS, BOOK 2

BY SIENNA SNOW

CHAPTER ONE

Amelia

"Amelia, could you at least pretend you want to be here and smile for the camera?"

I held in a groan as Sebastian Blake, internationally known photographer and a former high-school classmate, ordered me to smile for the twentieth time in the last ten minutes. Why the fuck I thought doing this magazine cover was a good idea was beyond me.

I was an Olympic gold medalist in taekwondo and a businesswoman, not a seasoned fashion model.

I shifted my shoulder, trying to roll the stiffness from it.

"Dammit, Amelia, stay still. I thought Greeks were made of sterner stuff. I will never understand how you could train for hours and bring home a gold medal, but you can't handle a photo shoot. I didn't fly all the way to Greece for the crap you're giving me."

"Bite me." I glared at Sebastian. "You tell me how you feel after hours of standing in the same unnatural poses. Plus, I'm an American like you, and we're delicate."

Sebastian snorted and handed his camera to his assistant before asking, "Are you saying I'm weak?"

"Aren't you the one who nearly had a temper tantrum because your legs hurt from standing too long in gym class?"

"We were in tenth grade, and I had a football injury. You're never going to let me live that down."

"You started it." I smirked.

"Point taken." Sebastian glanced around the room and said, "Let's everyone take a break."

I could almost hear the collective sigh of relief from the crew as they filed out of the studio.

"And get this woman an energy drink or something. Wonder Woman here is definitely not living up to her name," Sebastian added for good measure, knowing it would annoy me.

"You only wish you had my skills."

"I do, but I also know when to take a break. If I could get you to relax, then you'd be my perfect woman."

"Everyone can't be good at everything," I heard someone say from behind Sebastian, and my heart immediately lightened.

"Penny. Thank God. Are you here to rescue me?" I slid my feet off the chaise I'd sat on for the last forty minutes.

Persephone Kipos had been my best friend since childhood and was all-around the most amazing woman I'd ever known. She was the mastermind chemist behind Firewater, the whiskey that had taken the world by storm and made both of us filthy rich. Her for her incredible genius, and me for my initial investment in her labs.

She was also about to marry one of the sexy-as-sin Lykaios brothers, who ran dozens of entertainment and hotel venues throughout the world.

"Nope. You committed to this. Therefore, you have to see it through."

I sighed. "Well, I hope you at least brought me a shot of ouzo, or something with alcohol."

She smiled and gestured to someone behind her. "No, I brought you something even better. Though there's a chance he could give you a cavity from all his sweetness."

"Mama." My son, Christopher, ran toward me and engulfed me in a tight hug. His striking blue eyes shimmered up at me, making my heart clench.

God, he looked so much like his father.

"You weren't supposed to be back until tomorrow."

I beamed down at my beautiful boy's face. At a little over nine, he was on the cusp of transitioning from a little boy and to a teen, and soon he may not enjoy these hugs as much.

I glanced at Penny, giving her a grateful nod. Her phone rang, and she turned, leaving me with Christopher.

"*Yia Yia* Marie said you don't like to take pictures and I was the only one who could make you smile."

"She was right. You are my heart. Come." I patted the sofa next to me. "Climb on."

He jumped onto the cushions in the way only kids could get away with. He settled into my lap, and I couldn't help but savor the comforting scent of my baby.

"Stay just like that." The clicking of Sebastian's shutter echoed into the quiet room. "This is the first genuine smile I've seen all day. That boy has you wrapped around his finger."

"Yes, he does."

Christopher grinned up at me, and I couldn't help but kiss his forehead.

For the next twenty minutes, Sebastian held Christopher and me captive, and to my surprise, I had more fun than I'd had all day. My son had a way of getting me to relax, with silliness and laughter, just like his Papa had.

I quickly masked the pain that hit my heart as I thought about Stavros. It had been nearly two years since he'd died in a boating accident, and I missed him desperately every day. He'd been my rock when I'd found myself pregnant at eighteen with no idea what to do. He'd jumped to marry me and claim another man's child as his own. He was so much more than I'd deserved.

Especially since he wasn't the man I dreamed of at night or wished for with the heart of the eighteen-year-old who'd thought she'd met her soulmate.

"You're free to go." Sebastian's voice snapped me out of my thoughts.

"Thank God." I stood, helping Christopher down, and stretched my arms above my head to work out the kinks in my back.

"Mama, can I go to Peter's house? He has a new Lego set that he wants me to help him build. *Yia Yia* said if you were okay with it, she would drop me off at his house and then bring me home before bedtime."

"I suppose it is acceptable since you weren't supposed to be home until tomorrow. But remember, first thing in the morning, you have homework to get done for school."

He frowned. "I know. Why do the teachers give homework during the last weeks of school?"

"Because they enjoy torturing you." I ruffled his hair and then pointed to my mother. "There's *Yia Yia*. Go have fun."

My mom took Christopher's hand and led him out of the studio, leaving me to find Penny before we headed to my villa.

"I can't believe you're going to work with him after all he did to you. Are you sure you know what you're doing?" Persephone asked. About five months ago, my management company, Thanos Sports, had announced that our prized fighter Apollo Regalia was scheduled to take on Hugo Davis in an MMA heavyweight pay-per-view fight in Las Vegas.

The news wasn't what annoyed Penny, it was the fact Collin Lykaios had just signed on as Apollo's main sponsor.

Collin wasn't her favorite person, and up until last year, he wasn't mine either. The man had orchestrated the destruction of my relationship with his son. But then again, if he hadn't forced me to leave Pierce, then I'd never have married Stavros or had almost ten beautiful years together.

"Yes, I know what I'm doing. Besides, I could say it's your fault I made this deal in the first place."

She frowned. "Explain to me how this is my fault?"

"Aren't you the one who suggested I should look at other venues outside of Europe for my athletes?" I picked up a tumbler filled with ouzo, took a sip, and gazed out toward the Aegean Sea off the coast of Athens, Greece.

"I didn't mean come back to Vegas or join forces with Collin Lykaios."

"You're just biased against him since you're about to marry Hagen."

In a matter of months, Penny would marry the eldest one of Collin's estranged sons. Hagen was supposedly the darkest and most dangerous of the three brothers. I knew how wrong the assumption was. Hagen had made choices based on what life threw at him, but he was probably the least scary of the three Lykaios offspring. Hagen worshipped the ground Penny, or Starlight, as he liked to call her, walked on.

Pierce, on the other hand, was volatile by nature.

"No, that's not true. I told you Hagen and Collin had come to a peace. They're slowly working on their relationship."

"Then what's your problem?"

"Collin is Christopher's biological grandfather. Aren't you afraid he's going to find out you had Pierce's baby?"

It was something I'd feared every day since I gave birth to Christopher, but I wasn't going to tell Penny that. Besides, with Stavros gone, it was time to face the truth.

Pierce had a right to know about Christopher.

"No."

"Whatever. You're such a liar."

"I'm serious," I said defensively. "As far as the world knows, I was seeing both Pierce and Stavros at the same time. No one besides you, my parents, and Stavros knew I was pregnant before I married him, and I'd assumed you thought Christopher was Stavros's from the beginning."

It wasn't until last year that Penny revealed that she had always known Pierce was Christopher's father.

"I hate that you let everyone think you were an eighteen-year-old who slept around."

"Well, it was better to let the world believe I was the whore of the sporting world than have my father fired and mother deported."

Which had happened anyway. But Stavros had stepped in to help my parents settle back in Greece.

"And that's my point. How the fuck do you forgive the man who essentially destroyed your life?"

"Because he came to me and begged for my forgiveness. He's a broken man. It took a lot for him to face me and admit all his wrongdoing. He even went to my parents. The Collin of the past would never have come down from his pedestal to admit his mistakes."

"Wait." Penny sat up and gaped at me. "Say all that again."

I set my glass on a nearby table and decided to give her the story. "Last year, when I was in Ireland promoting Apollo's latest match, Collin asked to meet with me. He sent a note through my security detail saying he wanted to make amends for the pain he'd caused me."

"Well, that makes complete sense—that was the same time period when he and Hagen began to talk again."

"At first, I was hesitant. I hadn't seen or interacted with him since the night he told me I had to pick between my parents and Pierce. But then I learned he had visited my parents. If they could find it in their hearts to move past the deeds of ten years ago, so could I. Therefore, I called him and agreed to meet for tea."

"Are you sure it wasn't temporary insanity?" Penny interjected.

"Whatever it was," I continued, "I met with him and was surprised to find a very different man than I'd known ten years earlier. He was genuinely remorseful and knew what he'd done was unforgivable. He told me he caused me so much pain in order to protect Pierce and me. He only hoped one day he could make amends."

I never understood how breaking Pierce and me up helped protect us, but there were so many things I hadn't been able to grasp at the time everything went down. Instead of questioning my situation, I ran. Well not ran, but escaped into Stavros's world. A place I never truly fit into but gave me the security I needed.

A look passed in Penny's eyes that made me pause and say, "What? You know something."

Her gaze went to mine. "I can't tell you the details because it isn't my story to tell, just know it's true. He broke his relationship with his family in order to keep them safe."

"I didn't question him about it. I accepted his apology and decided to move on. Stavros taught me to let go of my anger years ago."

I remembered the lengthy discussions I'd had with Stavros. He'd gotten me to see perspectives I'd never considered. The man had deserved so much more from me than I had given him.

"He truly was an amazing man." Penny set her hand on mine. "Go on. Finish the story."

I inhaled deep, pushing back the sadness. "It wasn't until two months ago that we talked again. Apparently, Apollo had endeared himself to Collin over pints of Guinness while in Ireland, and Collin wanted to sponsor him in an international heavyweight fight. So, at the end of summer, Apollo Regalia and Hugo Davis will go head-to-head for the highest purse in MMA and boxing history."

"With Hugo under Pierce's management company, you're going to have to face the past."

"I know."

"And you're okay with that?"

"It's what's best for Apollo's career. My personal feelings have to be put aside."

"Okay, I'll buy that, but I see a few problems I think you're conveniently trying to ignore."

I crossed my arms. "And they are?"

"First, you're still in love with Pierce."

I opened my mouth to argue, but Penny cut me off. "I know you loved Stavros. I'm not trying to diminish what you felt for him or hurt you, but you never loved him the way you loved Pierce."

I held in a wince and felt a wave of guilt. She was right. I may have been a stupid teenager, but what I'd had with Pierce was never duplicated with Stavros.

Stavros and I had a friendship that developed into love. With Pierce, it had been all-consuming passion and a need I couldn't explain.

"It was teenage love. I grew out of it. I'm a mother now and don't have time for the past."

"That brings me to the second problem—Christopher. The instant anyone takes a good look at him, they're going to know Stavros isn't his father. Here in Europe, no one knows better. As Christopher grows, he looks more and more like Pierce. The second he steps foot on US soil, especially Vegas, it'll be obvious that Pierce and Christopher are related."

"I know." I pinched the bridge of my nose. "I'm hoping that since Christopher won't come to the US for at least five weeks after I get there, I can devise a plan to keep him out of the spotlight."

"Too late."

I frowned. "What does that mean?"

"You just did a mother-son photo shoot. Sebastian got some great pictures of the two of you, and there's no doubt in my mind that those are the ones he'll use. Christopher's face is going to be on the cover of *Vogue*, the European and American editions."

My stomach dropped, and a fear I hadn't felt since I

first found out I was pregnant filled my body. This was not how I wanted Pierce, or anyone else, to find out.

"Ame, it'll be okay. We'll figure something out."

I stayed quiet for a few moments and then took a deep breath and said, "I should have known better than to think any business with a Lykaios would be easy."

"This was in the making for a long time. Now you need to get to Pierce and tell him the truth before he finds out some other way."

CHAPTER TWO

PIERCE

"Hey, asshole. You better show up today." My brother Hagen's voice came over the phone the second I answered.

I pulled into a parking space outside of a giant warehouse on the outskirts of Vegas and turned off the engine. The last thing I wanted to do today was meet with my brothers, Hagen and Zack, for our weekly debriefing.

I was swamped with too much shit for a break. I had three contracts to review for amateur boxing matches, a racing event to negotiate, and most of all, I had to organize the final details of the heavyweight MMA bout between the European champ and my guy.

I wasn't trying to say my brothers were slackers, but I had deadlines that they didn't.

You see, my brothers and I ran Vegas. Well, the media liked to say we did.

At a young age, we'd joined forces and created HPZ Holdings, an entertainment and pleasure conglomerate that very few people could rival. Hagen ran anything and everything to do with Vegas nightlife. My talents lay in sporting events, from track and field to heavyweight fights. And my baby brother Zacharias, or Zack as we called him, was the gambler of our trio. He handled all casinos, hotels, and resorts.

"Yeah, yeah. I'll be there. It's not like I've ever missed before. And for the record, my business endeavors are the reason you made millions last week." I opened my door and was immediately hit by the sweltering desert heat.

Fuck, it was hot out here.

"Cry me a river. Without me, you'd be a washed-up swim instructor."

"Washed-up, my ass," I said as I strode toward the warehouse.

In the back of my mind, it always stung to remember the past. I'd worked so hard to regain control of my life. Hell, it was a daily struggle even now. There was only one time where I could remember that a simple touch from a delicate hand could calm the rage that boiled inside me because of the circumstances I lived in.

"Don't let those six gold medals get to your head. I'm bigger and can still kick your ass. Show up. It's important."

"I said I'll be there. I'm going to check up on Hugo's training, and then I'll drive over."

I hung up the phone and punched in the access code on the keypad to unlock the metal doors of the building.

"Hey, boss. Hugo just got back from break. He's in the ring practicing with Jeremiah."

I nodded to one of my facility trainers and headed into the central area of the gym.

The second I caught sight of Hugo, I smiled. This boy was going to make me proud. He was two hundred sixty pounds of honed muscle. He took direction well and used his head.

Now I only hoped he wasn't too starstruck by the idea of fighting his idol, Apollo Regalia, to kick his ass.

At near thirty, Apollo was five years older than Hugo and with years of experience, having started his career at the age of fifteen. He also had a bulldog for a manager. A woman who looked too fragile to handle the business but wouldn't hesitate to clock you in the nose for underestimating her.

I clenched my jaw.

If Hugo won, it wouldn't be just a victory for him but a fuck-you to the woman who, with a few choice words, had destroyed the heart and career of a nineteen-year-old swimmer.

I knew this match shouldn't be personal, but Amelia Nephus Thanos owed me for the hell she'd put me through.

On top of everything, she'd joined forces with the one man I'd washed my hands of years ago—Collin Lykaios. He may be biologically my father, but it was Hagen who'd stepped in when everything had imploded.

My phone rang again, snapping me out of my thoughts.

I pulled it out of my pocket and answered, "Yeah. What do you want?"

"Well hello to you too, shithead," Zack said. I could almost see him shaking his head at me. "I'm just making sure you're coming to the meeting."

"I already told Hagen I'd be there. What's so important that both of you are on my ass?"

"It's something you need to hear in person."

"That sounds ominous."

"It is. Your life's about to turn upside down."

An hour later, I walked into Ida, relieved to be out of the sweltering sun.

The Ida was the newest casino-hotel in HPZ. It was the most modern of our properties, catering to a younger, affluent demographic.

Hagen was the brother who oversaw the management

of the property, and because of this, there was a wicked edge to the atmosphere of the resort, echoing Hagen's personality. He was the one with the dark past but the brother who would do right by anyone he encountered. It was a kind of yin-yang thing with him.

The hotel was buzzing with people everywhere for such an early hour. But then again, Ida had operated at capacity since the grand opening six months earlier.

I greeted various managers as I made my way to the private elevator leading to Hagen's penthouse.

A few minutes before I'd arrived, Zack had sent a text saying not to go to Hagen's office but to go instead to his penthouse. Something about making sure we had complete privacy for our discussion without any chance of others overhearing.

I wondered where Hagen had stashed Penny if he wanted us to be alone. Penny was probably at the lab in her distillery concocting some new spirit.

Hagen shared his place with his fiancée, Persephone Kipos. Penny, as we called her, was the exact opposite of Hagen's dark, brooding ways. She was energy and laughter and daring, everything Hagen needed. No matter how hard he seemed to the world, he was the most sensitive of the three of us. I was forever grateful to Penny. She had given him the love he'd always wanted and never thought he'd deserved. She believed in him, even when he didn't believe in himself.

My phone buzzed again, flashing Zack's number.

"Seriously, man," I said, not hiding the irritation in my voice, "I'm about to come up the fucking elevator. Whatever you idiots have to tell me better be good. Do you realize how much shit I have to get done before the press conference next week?"

"You'll understand when you get here."

He hung up, and I entered the elevator.

The second I arrived at Hagen's penthouse, Zack pointed to the coffee table.

Hagen frowned at Zack. "Could you let the man walk in the door first?"

"It's better to let him know first before we have a nuclear explosion."

"Very funny, asshole," I muttered and moved to the table, freezing as I took in the cover of the upcoming issue of *Vogue*.

The headline read: "Amelia Nephus Thanos: Olympian, Sports Mogul, and Mother."

Under it was a picture of Amelia, in a Grecian-style one-shoulder silver gown, and her son.

God, she was beautiful. Her body was still toned in a way only an athlete who trained every day could achieve, and her long, black hair was styled in big waves instead of the ponytail I'd wrap my hand around.

I remembered spending hours staring into her amber-gold eyes as we'd discussed our dreams and the future.

She'd been my best friend. I'd shared all my pain with her, and she'd listened. She given me an outlet for the chaos of my life. She'd allowed me control in a way that no other women, no matter how hard they tried, could ever emulate.

In return, I'd given her the freedom to let go from the strict life she lived and the expectations she'd had to meet.

My gaze moved to the dark-haired boy in her lap, and my heart skipped a beat. Picking up the magazine, I traced the boy's face. He had lips the exact shape of his mother's on a face that looked too much like the one I saw in the mirror every morning. Then I noticed the wooden carving in his hand—it was one of the very pieces I'd played with as a child. A miniature Poseidon with a chip on its arm.

How had he gotten my favorite toy from childhood? Who would have given Amelia something like that for her son? Collin? Hell if I knew.

I studied the photo longer and couldn't deny the truth of what I saw.

Amelia had kept my child from me.

Why hadn't I noticed before? We'd always used a condom, so I'd assumed Amelia's baby couldn't be mine. And I'd been so devastated when one minute she was head over heels in love with me and the next she was dropping me for a much older Greek playboy.

Over the years, I'd seen pictures of Amelia's son, Christopher, but nothing had made me suspect I was his father. Then again, my mother had said I looked exactly like her in the beginning and then turned into a miniature version of Collin around the time I turned seven. And Christopher was only a little over that age.

"She let another man claim my son." My voice shook with anger as a lump formed in the pit of my stomach.

That was when I noticed an envelope tucked into the pages of the magazine. Pulling it out, I read the writing on the outside.

To Pierce Lykaios

Important. Read immediately.

From Collin Lykaios

My father had spent the last six months trying to get my attention with calls and messages. I'd ignored every one of them. The man had turned his back on me—hell, he'd turned his back on all of his sons. Instead of protecting us, he'd thrown each of us out as soon as it was legally possible.

If it hadn't been for Hagen, I would've never had the funds to train for the Olympic Games. Because of Collin, Hagen had to work for Draco Jackson, a Japanese mobster, doing God knows what. Because of him, Zack had to drop out of college to work, leading him to underground gambling rings and nearly getting sent to jail. Because of him, we boys missed spending the last years of our mother's life with her before she died of cancer.

The man was dead to me. It was better to pretend he didn't exist than unleash the rage I worked so hard to control on him. The fact Hagen had made amends with Collin didn't lessen how I felt.

"What did Collin have to do with this?" I asked through clenched teeth, failing miserably at keeping the indifferent attitude I'd perfected when discussing Collin around Zack or Hagen.

Hagen walked up to me, handing me a large tumbler filled with Firewater Incognito, the reserve cask of Penny's whiskey. "Drink this and then read the letter."

I shot back the whiskey and then grabbed the envelope, pulling out the paper inside.

Pierce,

I understand your hate and distrust. I deserve every ounce of it. You and your brothers suffered because of my failings. If I'd been a stronger man, if I'd been a better man, then none of you boys would have had to pay for my debts. Just know, it was all to protect you.

With that said, I did something to all of us, but especially you.

I thought I was protecting your future and career. You were so wrapped up in Amelia Nephus that you couldn't see anything but her. You both were still children in a relationship too adult for either of you to handle.

The reason she left you was that I forced her hand. I made her choose between you and her family.

At the time, I didn't know she was pregnant. It wasn't until I met with her in Ireland six months ago that I realized that her son Christopher wasn't Stavros Thanos's son but yours. She has no idea that I know. It is something the two of you will have to work out.

I'm so sorry I destroyed your chance to be a father.

Do not blame Amelia for her choices. She was innocent in all of this. She's a good woman. And for some reason, she forgave me.

I can only hope one day you can do the same. Not just for this but everything.

Collin

I stared at the letter for a few more minutes as my mind reeled from what Collin had written. Without a word, I stalked through the balcony doors of the living room and toward the ledge wall overlooking the Las Vegas Strip. Day or night, the area boomed with activity, and in a blink of an eye or the roll of the dice so many lives turned upside down. It looked like I was no exception.

I am a father.

I ran a hand roughly through my hair.

Christ. What the fuck was I going to do?

The world believed my son belonged to another man. A dead man, who from all accounts was loved and respected by everyone he knew.

Anger began to boil over. It didn't matter that Collin had made her leave me. She should have told me she was pregnant. But instead, she married another man within weeks of breaking things off, and on top of it, she let him raise my son, give him his name, and teach him things that were my right to do.

Shit.

I gripped my hair tight before releasing it.

I should have thought about the possibility.

What the fuck was I going to do? She lived in Greece, and Christopher had a life there.

Wait a second. Penny was just there last week. She had to have known. She was Christopher's godmother.

She'd helped keep my son from me. She was my sister in all but blood, and this was how she betrayed me. The hell I was going to let Hagen marry someone like that.

I turned and walked back into the penthouse.

I pushed past Hagen and rushed up the stairs leading to her home office. "Where's Penny? Where is your Starlight?"

"She's not here."

"Get her here," I ordered as I rushed back down. "She had to have known. All these years, she helped keep my son from me. What kind of person does this to people she claims as family? Does Penny have any loyalty? Are you sure she's worth marrying?"

Almost immediately, I realized my mistake in asking

the last questions and braced for the punch I knew was coming.

Hagen grabbed me by my shirt collar before my foot hit the last step and landed his fist into my jaw.

Zack pushed between Hagen and me, blocking the second jab that would have definitely left me with a black eye.

I collapsed to the ground as dizziness filled my head.

Fuck.

I'd forgotten how hard Hagen hit. I wasn't a small man by any means and could take on the best of them, but Hagen was the biggest of us, and with the years working as Draco's enforcer, he knew how to make every interaction count.

"Listen up, asshole. I get you're angry. You have a right to be. But you will never, ever disrespect Penny again. She is ten times the person you could ever be."

I rubbed my jaw and glanced at Zack, who didn't look any happier with me. "You deserved it. Penny's loyalties are with her only best friend since childhood."

"We've known her since she was in pigtails." I rubbed at my jaw and tried to work the pain away.

"It doesn't even compare." Hagen loomed over me again.

"She had to have told you," I accused.

"We only found out this morning when the envelope came. The magazine hasn't even hit the stands yet."

"So she kept this from you too?"

"Looks that way. She has no idea that we know. And we will keep it that way until I get a chance to talk to her. You will not mention any of what you learned outside of this room. Do you hear me?"

"Why? It's not as if she's as loyal to you as you believe."

Hagen clenched his fists and jaw. "Because this is between you and Amelia. It was her job to tell you. Knowing Starlight, she wouldn't have even told Amelia that she figured it out."

I took the hand Hagen offered me to stand.

I rubbed a hand down my face and winced when my fingers grazed my chin. "So you expect me to pretend that I don't know any of this?"

"Yes." Zack walked up, handing us fresh glasses of whiskey, and said, "She had to have been aware it would get back to you when she did the photo shoot. Give her a chance to explain. Christopher is ours by blood, but on record he is Thanos's and therefore Greek. That makes him an heir to a shipping fortune as well as Amelia's company. If you don't want Amelia to take her son and go back to Greece, you better play nice."

"Bullshit. That boy is as American as they come. Both his parents are American."

"You are so fucking hard-headed. Let me make this clear to you. If you want even a small chance of having a relationship with Christopher, then you'd better play nice with his mother."

"I'll play nice, all right. I'll make her fall in love with me again, and then when she least expects it, I will take my son back. No court in this country will let Christopher leave with all the red tape I plan to wrap around Amelia Nephus Thanos."

CHAPTER THREE

Amelia

I yawned as I entered the training facility Collin had built for my athletes behind his newest casino resort, the Cypress.

It was state of the art with six training rings, a giant weight room, and locker rooms that would give five-star spas a run for their money.

When Collin had shown me the plan for the building, I'd thought he'd lost his mind. It was way too much expense for something that would only be used for a few months. But Collin just smiled and said it could be an incentive for me to move my operation to the states.

The man I knew now was nothing like the one that had forced me to leave his son. The Collin of today seemed a bit broken and very lonely. He still was the cunning businessman he'd always been but with a softer, more gentle edge.

I released another yawn and shook my head, trying to clear the sleepiness. I glanced to my side and felt like growling when I noticed the three people comprising my security detail looking fresh and alert. I needed some of what they had. There wasn't an ounce of grogginess on them, and we'd been on the same flight. I guessed it was part of their job to be focused and wide awake.

It had taken me years to get used to having personal protection, and then a few more to stop noticing them as I went about my daily life. But I'd learned it was part of being a member of a well-known and uber-wealthy Greek dynasty.

"Still jetlagged?" Henna Anthony said as she walked up to me with a large cup of coffee.

Henna was Collin's right-hand woman. She pretty much ran his empire. She also happened to be Penny's first cousin and one of my closest friends.

"You're a lifesaver." I grabbed the hot cup and chugged the liquid heaven.

When I finished, Henna lifted a brow at me in amusement.

"Do you ever have a hair out of place?" I studied Henna's perfect designer outfit. "It's six in the morning, and you look like you walked off the pages of a magazine."

She lifted her wrist to look at her watch. "It's closer to seven. And to answer your question, I'm only dressed like this because I had a video conference with an investor in Indonesia. Differing time zones suck."

"Believe me, I know. Are we still on for tonight?" I asked. "I'm desperate for a night out. The last time I had any non-work or mom time was when Penny and Hagen had their little spat, and I took her to Ibiza to let loose."

"I doubt you did any letting loose. From what Penny told me, you orchestrated the adventure to get Penny to the club Hagen named for her so they could reconcile."

I sighed. "It was the least I could do for always being there for me. Penny deserved her happily ever after."

Unlike me. I'd fucked up any hope of that when I broke up with Pierce. Then I'd thought I'd gotten a second chance with Stavros, but it hadn't lasted.

Henna set a hand on my back. "You'll find love again too, Ame. Stavros wouldn't want you to stay single forever."

I gave her a weary smile and shook my head. "No. Love isn't in the cards for me. The best I can do is eventually find someone who I enjoy being with."

The thought of another relationship was something I hadn't even wanted to consider. At twenty-eight, I knew I was too young to say that I'd never date again. But the second I'd stepped on US soil, I felt the past with Pierce haunt me. I had to sort out the future with him and our son before moving on with another man.

"Maybe it's time you played with a new deck. Sometimes when one set goes cold, it's time to grab another one to play with."

"So speaks the poker shark."

"I'm serious. You're too young to live in the past. I am going to make it my mission to find you a Mister Right, or at least a Mister Right-Now."

Before I could respond, the head of my training team, Emery Gustav, approached.

"Boss, Selena is down with a cold and won't be here to spar with Neya."

It made no sense why he was telling me this. We had multiple alternatives to work with Neya, especially since we would have four fighters debuting in the women's matches the day before the main event.

Then it hit me.

"Are you implying what I think you're implying?"

A sheepish grin touched his lips. "You were complaining that you needed to burn off the jetlag. Coffee won't do anything close to what a few rounds in the ring can."

"You can't be serious. I'm a promoter, not a professional MMA fighter. Plus, Neya will kick my ass."

The last time I went head-to-head with a champion

was when I'd won my gold medal, and that was in taekwondo.

"Tell me you don't think about getting in the ring and I'll tell you that you're a liar. Before you left the sport, you were training to transition to the MMA circuit." Emery glanced at Henna for support.

Great, they were going to gang up on me. Even when I was eighteen, I knew my future was tied to MMA and the potential there. I had hoped to create a more prominent women's presence in a sport dominated by men. I spent my free time away from Pierce learning other martial arts disciplines. Then my world turned upside down and that dream had disappeared for a new one.

"He's right, you know. What's the point of training every day if you aren't going to get in the ring again?"

I swear I was going to kick Emery's ass. He'd coached me in MMA since before I'd had Christopher. My sponsors had hired him to help me with my transition from taekwondo to mixed martial arts. Then, after I'd recovered from my high-risk delivery, he'd moved to Greece to continue my training and help me build my portfolio of athletes. No matter how good he thought I was, my time in the ring was to stay fit, not to actually spar with a professional who made her living in the sport.

"Let me repeat: Neya will kick my ass. There's a difference between training to stay in shape and for a match."

Henna draped a hand over my shoulder. "Will you do it for me? It'll be fun, and it's only a sparring match, not a real fight."

"Plus," Emery added, "you can see firsthand Neya's weaknesses and areas to work on."

I could admit Emery's idea had merit. Over the years, I'd wondered what it would be like to get in the ring again, but after having Christopher, my priorities had changed entirely. The thought of training nearly every day of the year for fights all over the world hadn't had the appeal it did before. The promotion business was my conciliation. I was still in the sports world without the commitment to hours in the ring. Plus, it was my one way to rebel against the role expected of me as a Thanos wife.

Much to the horror of the Greek elite, instead of yacht parties and jet-setting the world, I trained athletes and got my hands dirty.

"You know you want to." Henna batted her eyelashes. "Come on. Pretty please."

I laughed. "You're too much."

But her giddiness had me feeling the surge of excitement I'd get before matches in the old days.

"Does that grin mean you'll do it?" Emery shifted from foot to foot in his version of a happy dance.

"Fine. Let me get changed."

Henna squeezed me and kissed my cheek. "I'm so

happy. I've hoped to see you in the ring for years, and I get to today."

"You better be here to do all the work when I can't move tomorrow."

"Seeing you go toe-to-toe with Neya will be worth it."

P ierce

A round nine in the morning, I pulled into the lot behind the Cypress casinos and had to shake my head at the three security checkpoints I had to pass to get within a few feet of the Thanos training facility.

This was overkill, even for Collin.

After my blowup in Hagen's penthouse yesterday, I'd spent the day researching anything and everything on Amelia, Stavros, and Christopher.

I'd tapped Adrian Kipos, our resident super-sleuth hacker and Penny's younger brother, for the task. Adrian worked for my brothers and me as a security spymaster but on occasion did some research on the side when we wanted information but didn't want anyone knowing that we were looking into their private activities.

The fact I was pissed to holy hell at Adrian's sister had

no bearing on my relationship with the boy. As long as he worked for me and completed the tasks I assigned him, we were good.

According to Adrian's report, Christopher was a typical mischievous nine-year-old, who liked sports more than school. He loved Legos and building things and had an affinity toward swimming and soccer. He willingly trained for hours in the pool and had won nearly every swim meet he'd entered.

I couldn't help but smile. My son took after me.

Stavros and Amelia were anything but typical. They were essentially Greek media royalty. Known for being notoriously private, they never courted attention or fed into it. However, their supposed love story made for great articles.

The young Greek-American athlete who'd fallen for the charismatic and lonely Greek widower, only learning he was a shipping billionaire after their wedding. Now she was the widow who hadn't stopped mourning the love of her life.

I clenched my jaw at the bitterness that filled me.

If he was the love of her life, what the fuck was I?

Get it together, Pierce. Stick to the plan. Seduce her and make it so your son is permanently in your life.

I pushed open the door to my Porsche and walked to the building's entrance.

I passed two cars in the lot with a small decal in the

corner that I recognized. They were Japanese symbols representing the Yakuza, the organized crime syndicate that ran Japan's underworld.

Great, Draco Jackson had his boys here.

Draco was a well-known mob boss in Vegas with his roots tied to the Yakuza. He also happened to be Hagen's former boss and the man who was trying desperately to get back in Hagen's good graces. They had a falling out about six months ago, which devastated Draco in a way that surprised not only his heirs, but all of us. Draco was far from the touchy-feely type but with Hagen, he'd lost someone he considered a son and that devastated him.

The fact his men were here was his not-so-subtle reminder of the debt he wanted to collect on. About nine months ago, Penny had needed help finding out who killed her father. Hagen had used his connections with Draco to help get the answers. But in exchange for his aid, he wanted something from each of us brothers. Zack and I'd agreed to his extortion plan because we loved Penny like a sister. Hagen was in love with her, so that was a given.

My debt was ringside seats to the upcoming fight between Hugo and Apollo. The fact he had sent his men here was to remind me he was collecting.

As if I'd forget an obligation to the monster that all but ran organized crime in Vegas.

I flashed a badge to a guard blocking the doors. He stepped aside, and I walked in.

Immediately I heard the roar of a crowd cheering, and I followed the noise.

I recognized Henna Anthony. She was jumping up and down in her designer outfit, shouting and laughing. "Come on, Ame. Show the young'un how it's done."

Ame?

My gaze shifted to the right, and my cock immediately jumped, transporting me to twelve years earlier when I was seventeen and training for my first FINA World Aquatics Championships. This was the first time I'd stepped onto the world stage, and my coaches were determined to make me a national champion, which meant no summer vacations or fun.

After one particularly grueling day of training at the Buchanan Natatorium on the campus of the University of Nevada, I'd decided to see the current heavyweight taekwondo champion Kosmo Yadira practice, instead of head home as Collin had ordered me to do. Kosmo was a legend, and I loved watching him kick ass in the ring.

But instead of Kosmo in the ring, I found him training sixteen-year-old taekwondo phenomenon Amelia Nephus. She was the daughter of one of Collin's casino managers. I'd heard of her, and we happened to go to the same high school, but we'd never met in person.

She'd fascinated me from the start. She was always so focused and determined to win every match she entered. There was a control to her that made me want to see what she'd be like if she ever let go of the reins. It had taken me a month to convince her to date me. But when I had, my world had turned on its axis.

She'd become my anchor, my world outside of swimming, my safe place. Then she'd ripped everything to shreds.

Fuck. I should be over this. But knowing she'd kept my son from me and now seeing her, opened up the wound that had festered for the last decade.

The crowd grew louder, snapping me out of my thoughts and refocusing on the action in play.

She wore fitted shorts and a sports bra that cupped her large breasts perfectly.

God, she was in shape. Honed muscles defined her arms, legs, and abs. They bunched and flexed with each movement, showing her flexibility and strength.

She wasn't the pampered socialite I expected her to be after marrying a billionaire, but an athlete who'd turned her love into a thriving business.

I'd be in awe of her if I wasn't so pissed.

Who was I kidding? It wouldn't matter how hurt, angry, or mad I was, or the fact she'd married another man —I'd never stopped wanting her.

My cock grew harder as visions of fucking her against the wall of our dorms in the Olympic village filled my head. Sex with her had always been intense, and explosive.

She'd never shied away from exploring anything and everything I'd proposed.

Thinking back on some of the things we'd done made me shudder—bondage, paddling, erotic asphyxiation. We'd had no idea the danger we'd played with.

Now with years of training and understanding, I was an expert at the world of kink, and I planned to use all my skills to exorcise the need that haunted me to this very day.

Great, now I was going to walk around with a hard-on. I adjusted my shirt to cover my dick.

That was the moment when Amelia's opponent turned, making me freeze.

What the fuck? She was going against Neya Adams.

Neya was the most decorated female in MMA history. She had a background in judo, taekwondo, and jujutsu. Plus, she had to weigh a good thirty pounds more than Amelia.

Whoever sanctioned this was out of their fucking mind.

I moved into the crowd and stopped when I reached Henna. The surprise on her face would have made me laugh if I hadn't seen Amelia knock Neya back with a roundhouse kick to the chest.

At that moment, Emery Gustav rang a bell to call an end to the match. He was a legend for his skills as a coach and making champions out of the unlikeliest of fighters.

There were groans all around.

"Come on, man. It was getting good," shouted a stocky man on the opposite side of the ring.

"Yeah," said another person. "How often does the boss get in the ring? One more round."

Emery rang the bell again, but this time longer and a bit more obnoxiously. "That's the end of the entertainment. Time to get work done and earn your pay. If you don't like it, file a complaint with management."

Another round of groans filled the room as everyone dispersed.

Henna turned to me. "I'm surprised to see you here. Our meeting isn't for an hour."

"I wanted to see the facility without the pomp and circumstance." I wasn't lying when I said that.

My purpose was to get a behind-the-scenes look at the people and fighters when they weren't putting on their best faces. What I hadn't expected was to find the woman who tormented my dreams in the middle of a round of MMA.

"I bet you got more than you expected." There was amusement in her voice.

I studied Henna. She was a breathtakingly beautiful woman. Dark chocolate eyes that couldn't hide her emotions unless she was at the poker table, and intelligence that bordered on scary. Something she shared with her cousin Penny and her sister Anaya.

The only negative thing I could honestly say about Henna was her eternal loyalty to Collin Lykaios. But then again, he'd been the father to her that he should have been to his three sons.

"Does she get in the ring often?"

"No."

I lifted a brow and waited for her to elaborate.

"This was a one-off. It's the first time Amelia has publicly sparred since..." Henna trailed off.

I finished her sentence. "Since she was eighteen."

Of course, today of all days, she decided to have a sparring match. To remind me of the woman I'd loved and adored with every ounce of my being.

"What did you think?" Henna looked toward Amelia and Neya.

They were in deep discussion. Probably about areas of improvement and strengths.

"She still has the strength and skill. It's as if she trains as a fighter and puts in the hours every day."

At that moment, Amelia's gaze locked onto mine. Surprise and something familiar passed in her eyes. It was a punch to the gut, as all the emotions and need I'd tried so hard to bury rushed forward, pushing back the anger and pain.

Amelia moved in our direction. She barely looked older than she had the last time I'd seen her. Though there were subtle changes in her body that I hadn't noticed earlier—she was lean, but her curves had filled out, especially her ass.

I could almost picture my hold on her hips as I fucked her hard from behind and she begged me to let her come.

Shit. Now I had another erection.

When she was a few feet from me, I saw the faint lines of stretch marks on her stomach. And my lust dimmed. My child had grown inside her, and she'd kept him from me.

"Hello, Pierce."

CHAPTER FOUR

Amelia

My stomach churned as I waited for Pierce to respond.

He still had the mysterious presence that had drawn me to him, even when we were young. But now it was more apparent, and there was a hard edge around him.

Physically, he'd grown from the six-foot-two lean-yet-lanky nineteen-year-old athlete into a honed, muscular man who filled out a suit as if it were second skin. Time had been very good to him.

In the middle of my match with Neya, I'd felt something shift in the room that had me hyperaware of everything and everyone around me. I was glad I hadn't seen him until I landed the roundhouse seconds before

Emery rang the bell or I'd have faltered. It was as if the second my foot touched back down to the mat and I turned, my gaze landed on him.

He watched me as he'd done in the past, with lust and promises of dark desires. My body had responded immediately.

He'd been the only man ever to garner that reaction from me. Not even Stavros could have heated my insides with a look.

A pang of guilt and disloyalty surfaced, so I refocused on Pierce.

"Hello, Ame."

God, that voice.

"Our meeting isn't until ten. We weren't expecting you." I took a towel Henna handed me and wiped my face and then my abdomen, not failing to notice Pierce following the movement of my hand.

His gaze lingered on my pebbled nipples.

"That was the point. I wanted to see how your team works when the cameras are away." He licked his lips and then frowned as he realized what he was doing.

Well, fuck. We were still attracted to each other. This was going to complicate things more than they already were.

"So, in other words, you wanted to spy on us."

His eyes lifted to mine and a slight grin touched his mouth. "You could say that."

God, that smile.

I had to keep my head on straight. I had to remember he was Christopher's father, and if I had any hope of telling Pierce the truth with minimal fallout, I couldn't act on my hormones.

"Though I can say the last thing I expected to see was Amelia Nephus in the ring."

"Amelia Thanos," I corrected and saw an immediate shift in his demeanor.

"I'm sorry about your loss. I heard Thanos was a great man."

I took a deep breath. I hated talking about Stavros.

Plus what could I say when Pierce was giving me condolences for the man he thought I'd left him for?

"Thank you." I looked at Henna who nodded, catching on that my emotions were going haywire, and then returned my attention to Pierce. "If you'll excuse me, Henna will get you settled. I need to clean up before the press gets here."

"If you'll follow me, Pierce. I'll take you to the cafeteria." Henna gestured to a hallway.

"Collin put a cafeteria in this place? This I have to see."

Pierce gave me one last once-over before joining Henna.

It took me twenty minutes to make it through the lingering crowd of crew and athletes wanting to discuss the match and their excitement at seeing me in the ring. I was grateful to all of them, but my heart was screaming for just a few minutes to digest what was happening to me.

I stepped into the bathroom adjacent to my private office and turned on the shower. Once the water reached my desired temperature, I stepped in.

The heat and force of the spray had me relaxing. I braced my hands on the wall and lifted my face into the water.

God. I hadn't expected Pierce to affect me as he had. His presence brought back desires and needs I'd long ago pushed away, things I could never have asked Stavros to do.

Stavros had been an amazing lover, always putting my needs before his. He treasured me. It had taken me nearly a year and a half after our marriage to take him to bed. He'd been patient and so careful with me. At the time I thought that was what I wanted—a sharp contrast to the all-consuming passion I'd had with Pierce.

Over the years, the gentle and sweet friendship Stavros and I had turned into love. Not the love I'd felt for Pierce, but one I knew would sustain me for the rest of my life. Stavros was truly my knight in shining armor.

But it wasn't meant to last. I could still remember the devastation I'd felt when the authorities came to our villa to tell me Stavros's boat was hit by a shipping vessel piloted by a drunk captain.

I'd gone numb, not wanting to believe he was gone. If it weren't for my parents, Penny, Henna, and Anaya, I wouldn't have been able to survive. My small tribe helped me cope with my loss and get my head on straight to care for Christopher as well as all of Stavros's businesses.

Businesses the Thanos family expected me to pass on to one of the male heirs of the family. Well, that wasn't true. Not everyone thought a woman should have control of the billion-dollar empire. My grandmother-in-law, Sylvia, was my biggest advocate. As the matriarch of the Thanos family, her word was law, and she wanted me to take over Stavros's role.

Her support meant the world to me and it had given me the encouragement to put the right people in place so I could focus on the business I'd created from the ground up, one that half the family still didn't recognize as worthy of the Thanos name.

I'd learned long ago I couldn't please most of my in-laws. I'd followed the rules, behaved the way I was supposed to, and it made no difference. It was when I stopped truly trying that I found my place.

Sports was my life. It was what I knew, and creating an enterprise where I could be in the middle of the action without sacrificing my time with Christopher was the perfect compromise.

Now here I was, full circle with the man, the city, and the business that started it all.

Seeing Pierce brought forth a longing I tried every day to suppress. I'd hurt him, hurt us, damaged his fragile trust that I'd always be there for him.

A tear slipped down my face. Was I disloyal to Stavros by realizing I never stopped wanting Pierce? Or lov—

I shook the thought from my mind. I couldn't go there.

I had to maintain a distance from Pierce and keep any and all interactions professional. It wasn't just my business on the line but Christopher too.

I had to arrange a time for Pierce and me to sit down and discuss the past and Christopher in a rational, adult way. After all, we were both near thirty and understood the importance of thinking things through.

Who was I kidding?

There was no doubt in my mind that Pierce was going to lose it. His emotions had always made him volatile. The fact he'd learned to control them wouldn't mean he'd rein them in with our situation. All I could hope was for him to be calm enough to agree to be introduced to Christopher slowly.

I was so fucked. There was no way I was going to come out of this unscathed.

My phone chimed, telling me I had to hurry up. I quickly washed my hair and then my body, wincing a few times as I stroked over areas where Neya had landed a hit. I stepped out of the shower, picking one of the tailored suits Henna had ordered for me, and then put on my game face.

By the time I walked out into the training room, I was back to the take-no-one's-shit sports promoter.

"There she is." Collin Lykaios came up to me and kissed my cheek. "I'm not sure if I should reprimand you or hug you."

"What did I do?" I asked, feigning innocence.

Collin was very protective of the women in his life, which included Henna, Anaya, and now me.

"I heard you gave the team some excitement today."

His deep blue eyes, so much like his son's and grandson's, gleamed with mischief. For a sixty-five-year-old man, he still possessed the devastatingly good looks and body of his youth but with refinement only time could polish. With Collin's genetics, Hagen, Pierce, and Zack were guaranteed to age well.

"You could say that." I smiled. "It gave me the opportunity to see the areas Neya could strengthen."

"What it did was give hermit over here a chance to show off all the training she still does in secret." Emery joined Collin and me.

"Whatever the reason, I'm grateful." Collin studied me and winked at Henna, who was approaching. "The morale of the team is high, and they have a buzz about them that wasn't there yesterday. It's good for them to see the people they work for have no problems getting their hands dirty.

But do me a favor. Next time, let someone else get punched. My heart nearly jumped out of my chest when I heard you were in the ring."

"I'll do my best not to scare you." I winked at him.

"Here, drink this." Henna handed me a green drink that resembled pureed grass.

I scrunched my nose. "Umm, no thanks."

Henna frowned and then ordered, "Drink it."

Before I could say no, a burly, larger-than-life man with jet-black hair and eyes just as dark came up to us.

Apollo Regalia was one fine specimen of male perfection. He was the current heavyweight champion in Europe and Asia with a following to rival some of the biggest movie stars. He trained hard and fought harder.

He viewed me as his adopted sister. We'd first met during my one and only Olympic Games, where he'd represented Spain in the men's heavyweight matches in taekwondo, and I represented the USA in the women's featherweight class. We stayed friends for years, and when I'd created my promotion and management company with Stavros, I'd brought him in as one of my athletes.

"I say fair is fair. You make me, Neya, and all the athletes drink that stuff after every match. Remember the email detailing the benefits of the wheatgrass protein shake to restore muscle strain and fatigue?"

"Apollo's right." Collin couldn't hide his amusement. "You have to set an example by walking the walk."

I grabbed the cup and muttered, "I never expected any one of them to buy the crap I wrote."

Holding my breath and praying I wouldn't puke, I took a sip.

Well, shit. This stuff tasted incredible. "Damn, that's good."

Apollo draped an arm around my shoulders. "Do you think we would drink something that tasted like real grass? We love you and know you want the best for us."

"But?" I continued his sentence.

"There is no way any of us would suffer through disgusting health drinks."

"I guess that explains the massive orders for the shake on the expense report." Henna grabbed the drink from my hand and took a sip.

Her eyes grew big, and she nodded her head. "I so need to add this to my diet."

I snatched my cup back and sucked down the rest of the concoction before tossing it into a nearby trash can.

"Time to smile pretty." Apollo released me and adjusted the belt on the robe he wore. "Did I tell you I hate all this bullshit pomp and circumstance?"

"Every single time we have to do any press," I responded.

We moved to the back doors of the facility to the press tent Collin had erected.

The moment we entered, my gaze locked with Pierce,

who was seated with Hugo Davis. There was an underlying lust to his stare that had me wanting to squirm. Instead, a tingle ran up my spine, and I couldn't help but shiver.

Of all the places to try that Dom stuff, he'd pick now.

"Is everything okay?" Henna asked from behind me.

"Yep." I walked up the steps of the stage and greeted everyone from one end of the long table, shaking hands until I reached Pierce.

"Hello again." I offered Pierce my hand.

He took it in his, and I nearly moaned. We hadn't touched since the last time he'd made love to me over ten years earlier.

"Hello, Ame."

My breath became a little erratic.

Dammit, Amelia, you're supposed to keep it together. Remember you're the ballbuster promoter, not Pierce's... Nope, not going there right now.

His lips twitched, telling me he'd caught my reaction.

I pulled my hand from his and introduced everyone with me before the press conference began.

The next hour flew by faster than I expected. The media loved Apollo and Hugo. They were so similar it was surreal. They were humble, spoke eloquently, and had the reporters eating out of their hands. The men had a mutual respect that gave them an endearing quality.

When they stood to do the usual scowling at each

other with their hands-up pose for the cameras, I wasn't the only one who was struck by how good looking the two fighters were. A person had to be dead not to notice.

"Thank you, everyone. We'll see you at the weigh-in," the press-conference moderator said.

I stood, glancing at my watch and avoiding the urge to look at Pierce's end of the table.

Henna slipped a hand into the crook of my elbow to keep me on the stage and put some distance between the rest of our team and us.

"Is it wrong for me to lust after both of them?" Henna whispered so none of the men around us could hear. "Can't you just imagine being the filling in an Apollo and Hugo sandwich?"

"Get your mind out of the gutter. Aren't you the woman who's all business, all the time with no room to deviate? This is business." I tried to give her a stern glare but couldn't hold it as a grin won out.

"I'm still a woman and can appreciate sexy man-candy."

I shook my head. I truly loved that Henna let down her hair with me. She was so controlled all the time that many mistook her as being cold and calculating. But in fact, she was one of the most easygoing and fun people I knew. "Can't argue with that."

"Speaking of man-candy. Penny has arranged a table at

Hagen's new club for all of us. I'm sure there will be plenty of celebrities to dance with tonight."

"Since when are you and the Lykaios brothers all chummy, chummy?"

"When your cousin is about to marry the love of her life, who happens to be one of them, you put aside the animosity. Now it doesn't mean I like all of them, but Hagen and Pierce aren't so bad."

"That means you have issues with Zack."

"He is the one Lykaios I'd be happy never to interact with. Ever. He wants to destroy Collin and doesn't shy away from letting anyone know." Henna clenched her jaw.

Henna and her sister Anaya were the daughters of Victor Anthony, a man who'd swindled nearly a billion dollars from his investors in one of America's most notorious financial scandals. Instead of taking responsibility, Anthony had committed suicide, leaving his family to take the fall, which included the seizing of all assets and death threats. Collin, who'd been a victim of the scheme, had protected the girls and their mother by moving them out of state and giving them new identities.

Because of this, Henna was loyal to Collin down to the core of her soul.

"The two of you are so much alike it boggles the mind."

"The only place we can coexist is during the private poker matches we enter with our high rollers. There we know the rules and get along just fine."

"It would serve you right if you ended up in bed together after one of those games."

She snorted, but the way she wouldn't look in my direction said she'd thought of the possibility. "Never going to happen."

"I believe you protest too much. Besides, Zack is hot."

"Why don't you focus on the Lykaios who was all but fucking you with his eyes today and leave me alone."

CHAPTER FIVE

PIERCE

Around midnight, I walked into Ida and headed to Nyx, the nightclub Hagen had designed around Firewater. I'd thought he'd lost his mind when he wanted to sink millions into the project based on a product that could be a fad, but his vision had been spot-on. Now, every rival club wanted to emulate Nyx.

The craziest part of the whole endeavor was that until Hagen and Penny got together, neither Zack nor I knew Penny was the creator of the internationally sought-after whiskey that tasted like it was aged for years but in fact was only months old.

Hagen had been in love with Penny since we were

kids, but he thought they could never be anything more than acquaintances because of his dark past working for Draco Jackson. It wasn't until Penny's brother, Adrian, who happened to work for HPZ, arranged a business lunch for Hagen and Penny that they finally acted on the attraction.

As I approached the club, I noticed the line to get in was twice the normal size. One of the bouncers caught my confusion, and he only shook his head in response before he said something into his earpiece.

"What the fuck is going on in there?" I asked Damian Riker, Ida's general manager, the moment I saw him.

"Mr. Lykaios, we have a bit of a celebrity situation in the club. Word got out that Apollo and Hugo are here."

Well, that was just great. Two guys who were supposed to be on opposite teams were partying it up together. I wasn't against them being friends, but it made for better ticket sales when there was a rivalry.

"Is security in place?"

Damian nodded. "We had it arranged when Ms. Kipos reserved the VIP section. No one without silver wristbands can access the area, and we implemented a second security check to verify names with Ms. Kipos's guest list."

"Are there any other guests up there?"

"Yes. Vivian James and Xander Caro with their respective groups. Both parties know Mrs. Thanos and understand the need for discretion."

It also helped that the two movie stars were having an affair and wouldn't want anyone knowing about it. Especially since the public thought they were with other people.

"Where's Hagen?"

Amusement passed over his face. "He's standing guard over his fiancée."

I couldn't help but laugh in return.

If there was one thing true about Hagen, it was that he was overprotective of Penny. The man had wanted her for so many years thinking he couldn't have her and that he didn't deserve her. Now that she was his, he wasn't letting go.

Once upon a time, I'd had the same thoughts about Amelia, but she chose to run instead of coming to me. I was well aware she'd been barely eighteen, but she was carrying my child and had kept it from me.

"Is Zack here?"

"Not yet. He went to meet some whales that arrived from the Middle East. You know how Mr. Lykaios is. Work comes first."

Or he didn't want to be in the same space as Henna Anthony. For some reason, those two had a hard time getting along. Maybe it was the fact they were so similar. Despite her poor taste in adoring Collin, Henna was a great person, at times a workaholic and a bit too driven, but someone who would walk through the fires of hell for the people she cared for.

"I'll head up." I moved in the direction of the hidden entrance of the club.

After taking two hallways and a set of stairs, I reached the VIP lounge. The music from the dance floors below blared into the space, keeping the nightclub atmosphere going.

As I stepped onto the floor, I came to an abrupt stop. Amelia, Henna, and Neya were all dancing together. It was obvious they'd had a few drinks, and their guards were down. Their movements were sensual and a bit erotic. I wasn't the only one mesmerized. Many of the club patrons on the lower level were watching them, as were Apollo and Hugo as they sat on the sofas, drinking. Apollo's gaze was focused on Neya, but Hugo's was on Amelia and Henna.

I clenched my jaw when he licked his lips, and counted to ten to calm the urge to punch him. I had to remind myself he was a normal red-blooded man watching beautiful women dance.

"Well, fucking hell," Zack said as he came up behind me.

His focus was locked on Henna. A crease formed in his brow. "If that boy doesn't stop eye-fucking them, I swear to God we won't have a man in the ring a couple of months from now."

Well, wasn't that interesting? Baby brother had a thing

for the enemy. Poor guy was in for a rude awakening if he ever got in a relationship with her. She wasn't his usual type. He had a habit of going for women he could handle and keep in their respective places. Henna was smart, funny, and took no one's shit.

"Are you referring to them as a whole or Henna? I'm not sure she'd appreciate your possessiveness. In fact, she'd probably stomp you into the ground."

"Fuck off. Why don't you worry about your baby mama."

Zack's words had me grinding my teeth and helped remind me that I was on a mission.

"I don't need to worry. She'll walk right into the trap I'm setting."

Amelia danced around Neya and Henna, laughing and singing to the song in the celebrity DJ's mix.

"I think seducing her is a bad idea. She's been through enough over the years. For Christ's sake, she just lost her husband."

"She kept my son from me and let another man raise him."

"She had her reasons. Give her a chance to come clean."

"She had over ten years."

"So seducing her is going to be payback? Then what? You break her heart like she broke yours? If you want any sort of relationship with your son, I'd take a step back."

At that moment, Amelia turned in my direction and our eyes locked. There was no alcohol haze in her gaze, only heat. She had never been able to hide her response to my presence.

My body instantly reacted, craving her touch, her mouth, her body.

"There's no going back. This morning, it took me less than ten seconds to know we still wanted each other. She knows as well as I do that it's inevitable we'll end up in bed."

"I doubt she's into your forms of proclivity."

"You don't know her at all." I smirked. "She wasn't only my first lay. She was my first submissive. I knew I liked kink from the very beginning. Amelia was the one who helped me explore it."

"The world she's lived in for the past ten years is pretty conservative. She could have changed."

"No, she hasn't. She may have turned down the need for it over the last ten years, but it never died. I plan to give her what she secretly craves and get what I want in the end."

"You're digging your own grave. I only hope you don't take us down in the process."

"I know what I'm doing." I moved toward Amelia.

Well, I hoped I did.

She watched me until I was almost a foot away from her. I held out a hand.

"Dance with me, Amelia."

A melia

My pulse accelerated as I stared at Pierce's outstretched hand. The single Firewater shot I'd downed had loosened my inhibitions enough to dance, but it hadn't dulled my wits. And I knew his request wasn't a question but a polite order.

I'd felt his presence the second he'd moved into the lounge. It had always been that way. Then when I'd turned, I'd nearly swallowed my tongue.

His wore a fitted black T-shirt, displaying the broad definition of his muscular shoulders, and a pair of dark denim jeans. Even after all these years, he had the physique of a swimmer. The only jewelry he wore was the Patek Philippe watch on his left hand. The one waiting for me to accept his offer.

"It's not a good idea." I licked my lips and saw his blue eyes move to them.

A tingle went up my spine, and my core spasmed.

Shit. I was in deep trouble.

"Of course, it is. It's not like I'm asking you to have sex

with me. Besides—" He paused as he grasped my hand and led me to the dance floor.

Then, he pulled me against him, laying a firm but gentle hand on my back, reminding me of the past. In the way he'd calm me when I was uncertain or needed reassurance, or after intense sex.

"Besides what?" My voice was breathy.

God, he smelled good.

He leaned in and whispered, "Besides, when I fuck you, it won't be because I asked you to but because you begged me to."

Everything in me trembled, and I was confident he felt it. He'd always had this uncanny ability to rattle me.

As the music changed, his palms slid to my hips, gripping them in the way that made everything inside me awaken. My nipples pebbled and my cleft grew slick.

His cock hardened, long and thick against my abdomen, adding to the desire burning in my body. The fact he wasn't shy about pressing it against me told me he wanted me to react.

We danced as we'd done so many times when we were younger—our movements in sync.

He released his hold on one hip to slide his hand upward until he held my rib cage, applying slight pressure.

My breath hitched as visions filled my mind of my arms bound behind my back and him fucking me in the same position he held me now.

"Are you okay?" He rubbed his stubble-covered cheek along mine.

He had to know what he was doing to my body.

When we were younger, I had no comprehension of the type of relationship we'd had. All I knew was that I had complete trust in Pierce knowing what I needed and giving it to me. He liked to control, and for some reason, I'd loved giving it to him.

It had taken me years to forget the freedom and pleasure I'd experienced in his arms. When I'd married Stavros, it took me so long not to feel like I was trapped in a cage of etiquette and old-world rules.

A pang of guilt hit me for even thinking that way about my life with Stavros.

He'd saved me when I had no idea where to go, and here I was comparing my life with him to another man.

I tried to step out of Pierce's hold, but he held me firm. "Pierce, please. This can't happen."

"I know you feel it. The urge to sink to your knees, the urge to bow your head and wait for my command."

I shook my head to deny his statement, but he cupped my jaw so I was looking into his lust-glazed eyes.

"You can lie to yourself." He ran a thumb over my lower lip. "But you can't lie to me. You may have suppressed your desires in your super-conservative life with your rich, older husband, but they're still there. The need to be owned. The need to submit. The need to be fucked hard."

A whimper escaped my mouth. He was right. I wanted it, needed it, but if I opened that door again, it could leave me in shambles when Pierce learned the truth.

At that moment, the flash of a camera had me pulling back and breaking free of Pierce's spell.

I glanced in the direction of the light to see Vivian James and Xander Caro taking selfies.

Without thinking, I went to grab my purse from the nearby sofa. I had to get out of here.

How could I be so stupid? I couldn't go down the rabbit hole again. Panic began to fill my chest.

I turned to leave but collided with Pierce's chest, clutching his shoulder to steady myself.

"Where are you going?"

"I have to go back to my hotel."

"Why?"

It took me a second to think of an excuse. "I want to call Christopher before he goes to school. If I leave now I can catch him." I glanced at Penny, who stopped dancing with Hagen to come over to me.

"Can you call our driver to take me back?"

There was a worried look on her face as her gaze went between Pierce and me.

Before she could respond, Pierce said, "I'll take her back."

"We all should go." Neya approached us and slung an arm over my shoulders. "It's late, and my manager is a stickler for me getting to my training sessions on time."

Pierce clenched his jaw, and I felt a sense of relief.

"Yes, I know her personally, and she is a taskmaster." I tried to make light of the situation, but the tightness in my stance gave away my true feelings. "Neya, stay. Tomorrow is your day off."

"Are you sure?" Henna came up now. "We don't mind calling it a night."

I felt Pierce's agitation rising and knew it was better to deal with him than cause a scene.

Back in the day, Pierce had a reputation as the bad boy of swimming, always mouthing off or being confrontational. It had taken a near disqualification from the US team to get his act in gear. He'd made a complete one-eighty and gone from out-of-control rich-kid star athlete to an ultra-focused, goal-oriented, and always-in-control champion.

That was around the time we'd met. The only time he'd ever slipped into his old ways was when he had confrontations with Collin or when his trainers would keep us apart so we could prepare for the Olympic trials.

"I said, I'd take..." Pierce trailed off as I set a hand on his chest, and immediately, his stance calmed and his focus moved to where I pressed against his shirt.

Dear God, it still worked.

He lifted his gaze to mine, making me realize he was as shocked as I was.

Quickly, I turned to the group. "It's okay. Pierce will drop me off at the Cypress. You guys have a good time. Let's go, Pierce."

No one argued as I walked toward the exit with Pierce close on my heels.

CHAPTER SIX

Pierce

I watched Amelia as she led the way through the back hallways of the club. The energy between us had shifted in a way I hadn't expected. When I'd strong-armed her into dancing, I'd felt lust mixed with the underlying anger of everything between us. Then, when she'd stepped between me and her friends, placing her delicate hand on my chest, I had a rush of calmness I hadn't experienced in over a decade.

One touch and the irritation eased.

Dammit. She wasn't supposed to affect me like this.

She remained quiet while my car pulled up, and then I helped her in.

The second the doors shut, she closed her eyes and leaned her head back, all but putting up a wall between us.

As I got behind the wheel, I noticed her face was ashen with a hard edge, as if she was braced for a confrontation.

We drove in silence for a few minutes before I couldn't take it anymore. I knew I was an asshole, and despite what my anger wanted me to do, I couldn't hurt her.

"I'm sorry."

She opened her eyes and stared at me. "For what, exactly?"

"For pushing you. For coming on to you so strong. I didn't expect it to feel so intense to be around you."

I hadn't expected one simple graze of her fingers to remind me of what she'd meant to me.

"Nothing can come of this, no matter how strong this attraction is between us. After the fight, I plan to return to Greece."

"I know."

She looked out the window at a group of partiers in a stretch limo dancing through the moonroof and then back at me. "Isn't it inconvenient to drive me to the Cypress?"

"Actually, the Cypress is on the way to my place."

"Your place?" she questioned.

"Yes. The Aegean is mine and it's down the street from the Cypress."

Her eyes grew big.

The Aegean was the casino-hotel known throughout

the world for its fountains. Everything was designed around the theme of water. It was a mix of modern and classical architecture. It was also the most award-winning property in the HPZ arsenal, much to Hagen's chagrin.

"Why do you have a hotel? I thought you were the sports god of the group? Don't they call you Master of Games?"

I nearly rolled my eyes. That name was so stupid. A few years ago, *Rolling Stone* did an article about Hagen, Zack, and me. They latched on to our Greek heritage and dubbed us the Gods of Vegas since we were three Greek brothers who'd estranged ourselves from our father. And then another magazine had done a piece on me, dubbing me the Master of Games because of my former athlete status and my sports promotion company.

"Each of us has a casino-hotel we run in addition to our other endeavors. Hagen has the Ida, Zack has the Aegis, and I'm in charge of the Aegean. The other properties are managed by trusted groups of men and women."

"I guess they are sub-deities." She smirked, and the shadows clouding her eyes disappeared.

"Very funny."

"You do realize that with all the names you three picked for your properties, it's no wonder they refer to you as the Greek gods. If you didn't want comparisons, I'd have decided on something less Greek."

"We like our Greek heritage. We're the first generation

outside of Greece, so what better way than to name things that we own after Greek places."

"Aegis isn't a place. It's the name of Zeus's shield."

"That's all Zack. It is a tribute to our Mama. She gave him an antique pendant of Zeus's shield right before she passed away. It was nearly a thousand years old and one of her prized possessions."

I hated thinking back on those days. We hadn't learned of Mama's cancer until she'd entered hospice. Hagen and I had been on our own for years by that time and were used to having limited contact with our mother. But Zack had been in his second year of college, barely twenty, and hadn't handled the situation well.

Mama had given Zack the pendant to remind him he was protected and loved.

Amelia sniffed as tears clouded her eyes and then asked, "Did you know she stayed in touch with me after we broke up? She'd come to see me every time she visited her family in Greece. She would bring presents for Christopher and a giant box for me containing my favorite American treats."

Now that was news. Mama had visited her sisters at least three times each year. But I never thought she'd visited the girl who'd destroyed my heart.

Why would she keep this from me?

I'd never know the answer to that question and a million others that I had for her. Mama was gone, and the only person who could possibly give me any resolution was Collin, and I was no way near ready to talk to him.

"One time she brought Christopher these little custom carved statues, telling me every Greek boy should know his mythology. At the time, I thought she was crazy. At barely a year, all Christopher would do with them was use the pieces as teething toys. It wasn't until a few years after she passed away that he truly played with them. Now, he's obsessed, never letting them out of his sight, especially this one of Poseidon with a chip on..."

"...the left arm," I finished, startling her. "They were mine. I accidentally broke a chunk off the wood when I tried to attach a sword to the piece."

We stared at each other, feeling the raw emotions before I turned my attention back to the road.

Pain shot into my heart. Mama had to have known or at least suspected Christopher was mine—that would be the only reason why she'd give him something I'd specifically saved to give to my own child one day.

"Pierce. There's something I have to tell you."

I held my breath, knowing what she would say. "What?"

She wrung her hands and took a deep breath.

"It's about..." Her words died as we reached the private entrance for the residential area of the resort.

The valet opened the door, and I nearly cursed.

Placing a hand over her arm, I stayed her before she could move.

"Keep going."

A flash of panic came over her face, and her breath grew uneven.

My heartbeat was drumming a marching beat as I waited for her to respond.

She released a sigh of resignation, and I felt a stab in my heart.

God, what was I doing? Was this how I wanted to hear that I was a father? In a fucking car, of all places.

Before I could tell her to wait to talk, she shook her head. "No. This needs to happen when I have a clear head, not when I've spent the night out."

I studied her. Her face was pale and dark circles rimmed her eyes. After a few seconds, I said, "When?"

"Soon. I promise soon." She stepped out of the car and hurried into the hotel.

Amelia

"Good morning, sunshine," I said into the phone with

my most cheery voice as I entered my suite and kicked off my heels.

"Mama!" Christopher's exuberant voice came over the line. "Three more weeks and we'll be there with you."

"I can't wait to see you, my sweet boy. But it's five more weeks."

"I forgot. Why can't we fly to America as soon as school finishes?"

I walked into the living room and dropped onto the couch, immediately pulling the blanket I'd thrown on the end over my feet.

"Because *Yia Yia* and *Pappous* have to close up the house and pack for the whole summer. That's a lot of work to get done. Plus, it will give you nearly two weeks to do nothing except play with your friends."

"*Yia Yia* says I can bring my Greek carvings. She said if I behave and don't talk back, she'll let me bring the whole collection."

"Wow, the whole collection. Isn't that nearly fifty pieces?"

"Yep. I have to put them in storage with our luggage, but she'll let me take three of my favorite pieces onto the plane."

I rubbed my chest, feeling the ache of the conversation I'd had with Pierce and the way I'd left things.

It was as if Pierce had known what I'd say. That meant

he had to have seen the pictures from the photo shoot and recognized the toy Christopher held.

I was sent advance copies of all the editions of the spread. Each had a slightly different pose, some with Christopher on my lap or sitting beside me. The one that would hit the stands in the USA had me leaning on the back of the chaise with my legs outstretched to show off my gown. Christopher was positioned against my shoulder, with his hand resting on my left arm and the figurine of Poseidon in the palm of the other. Only if someone inspected the picture could they have made out what Christopher was holding.

Christopher's chatter broke into my brooding. "*Yia Yia* said I can swim every day if I want to when we're in Las Vegas."

"That you can. The hotel we're staying at has twelve pools."

"Really?"

"Yes, really."

"You know what that means?"

"What?"

"You can watch me practice and give me pointers like you do your athletes. I can be one of them. And one day you can be my manager."

I smiled. This boy held my heart tight in the palms of his hands.

"I would love that."

"Did you know that *Pappous* Collin's son is Pierce Lykaios? Did you know he swam in the Olympic Games and won six gold medals? *Pappous* Collin promised to introduce us when I get to Las Vegas."

"*Pappous*? When did you start calling Mr. Lykaios that?"

I was not going to touch the subject of Collin's son.

"When we were in Ireland. Remember when I went to the park? He was there. He looked so sad as he stared at the ducks. I decided to say hi and make him smile by talking to him."

"Where was *Yia Yia*?"

"She was there. She told me it was good to make others smile."

Oh, did she? Mama and I were going to have a nice chat when Little Man wasn't around.

"I like him. He said I was the exact person who could cheer him up. He bought me ice cream. He made me laugh with all kinds of silly jokes. He told me not to call him Mr. Lykaios. He said it sounded too formal. I'm supposed to call him *Pappous* since he doesn't have any grandsons yet. Did you know he has horses and cows and sheep on a ranch he owns? I can't wait to go riding on a horse like a cowboy. *Pappous* Collin said he would teach me to ride as he taught his sons. I can't wait to get there."

I let Christopher continue to ramble and swallowed the anxiety bubbling up inside me.

I'd known what would happen when I let Christopher join the photo shoot. Now it was time to face the consequences of all my past decisions. First, I had to face Pierce, then it was only right to tell Collin. The man needed family, even if it was a grandson who lived an ocean away.

"Mama, will you let me ride horses? Please...pretty please? And I can't wait to go to that hotel with the roller coaster. I saw it on the Internet. And there's a moat with millions of fountains. I have to go there."

Deciding to change the subject and stop Christopher's stream-of-consciousness chatter, I asked, "How's your last week of school going?"

He groaned, effectively ending his excitement. "It's okay. I can't wait until I don't have to learn stupid Latin. I can speak Greek and English. Why do I need to learn Latin?"

"Because it makes you smarter, and knowledge is power. You can lose all your money and possessions, but you can't—"

"—lose your education," Christopher finished with an exaggerated huff. "I know. I just wish I was like Nickolas. He has a tutor and never goes to school. I want a tutor, then I'd never, ever, ever have to go to stupid school."

"Hate to break it to you, but a tutor is a teacher. And Nickolas's teacher lives with him in his house and goes everywhere Nickolas does. That means he has school year round and even on vacations."

I could almost see Christopher scrunch his face in disgust.

"Oh no, I don't want that."

"Figures." I couldn't help myself and laughed.

In the background, I heard a quick succession of Greek and expected my mom to take the phone any second.

"Mama. I have to go. *Yia Yia* wants me to put on my shoes so *Pappous* can take me to school."

"Okay, baby. I'll call you tomorrow. Give the phone to *Yia Yia*. I want to say hi."

"Bye, Mama. Love you."

"I love you too, sweetheart."

"*Yassoo*, Amelia."

"*Hi, Mama. So when did Collin meet Christopher?*" I responded in Greek, unable to hide my irritation. "*He told me all about* Pappous Collin *and his son who was in the Olympics.*"

"*That boy talks too much. I swear he cannot keep a secret for the life of him.*"

"*Mama!*"

"*What is the big deal? He looked so lonely by himself on the edge of the pond. There is nothing wrong with a little boy bringing some happiness with his joy.*"

I released a sigh. I couldn't fault her for having sympathy for the man. I felt the same way every time I was around him. The formidable and scary man of my past was gone. And in his place was a man full of regrets, wanting to make amends for all his wrongdoings.

"*I guess you're right. Christopher can put a smile on anyone's face.*"

"*Of course, I'm right. Don't question your Mama.*"

I shook my head at the indignation in her voice. "*I promise never to do it again.*"

"*Until the next time it happens,*" she muttered. "*Now, I want to know how you are.*"

I exhaled. "*I'm good. A little tired—it is past two in the morning here.*"

"*No. I mean how are you?*" She emphasized the "you" part. "*I know when you are upset.*"

"*I guess I am as well as I can be. At times it is like we never left and others, it feels like everything has changed.*"

"*I mean, how are you handling Pierce?*"

I shifted the phone. "*What is there to handle? He manages Hugo. I manage Apollo. End of story.*"

"*Amelia Christina Nephus Thanos.*"

I cringed hearing her use my full name. Well, I'd just pissed off my mother.

"*What?*"

"*Did you tell him that he is Christopher's father?*"

I sat up and prepared myself for a lecture. "*Not yet.*"

"*And why not? I will never understand why you continue to let him believe you were sleeping with him and*"

Stavros at the same time. Isn't it time to end the charade? Haven't you suffered enough?"

I hated thinking about how the media had eviscerated me when the news broke that I was pregnant. I was called everything from a child screaming for help to the whore of the sports world. My parents were my rock, pushing aside their super-conservative Greek beliefs and suffering through the scrutiny, while never leaving my side.

"Is that why you invited Rhea Lykaios to visit when I was pregnant? Did you tell her Christopher was her grandson?"

"You think I don't know you're trying to put the spotlight on me?"

I stayed quiet until I heard my mother huff and start talking again. *"I swear you are as stubborn as your Papa. Rhea was my friend, despite what her husband did to us. She never gave any indication she knew, but deep down I was positive she did. One thing Rhea was good at was keeping secrets."*

"Like?"

"It is not your concern. What you need to focus on is Pierce. He has a right to know the truth."

"Mama," I grumbled, *"I will tell him, but I have to get my bearings here."* All of a sudden my voice cracked and a flood of emotions erupted. *"It was so hard seeing him. And the worst part is I feel so disloyal to Stavros."*

"Oh, gliko mou, *love doesn't just stop. Pierce was your*

first love. Stavros understood this when he married you. There is no disloyalty in this situation."

"I really need a hug right now."

"Soon," she soothed.

"I love you, Mama."

"And I you."

There was loud chatter in the background, telling me Christopher was leaving. As soon as I heard the sound of the door closing, Mama returned.

"Now that the house is quiet, I need to tell you a story. Something I should have told you years ago. It will help you understand so many things from the past and the events that led to us returning to Greece."

CHAPTER SEVEN

PIERCE

"We need to talk."

I looked up at Hagen as he walked up to my desk and set his phone on top of the papers I was reviewing.

It was an article from an online celebrity news magazine with an image of Amelia and me from a few nights ago. My thumb was on her lower lip as she gazed up at me. There was intense emotion in her eyes, almost like the way she'd looked at me when I thought we were in love.

"So what? You were there."

"I thought you were just dancing. I was in the back

with Starlight. I didn't think you were trying to get in her pants."

"If she's willing, why are you bothered? It's not like I hid my plans from you, in the first place."

"Don't fuck with her, Pierce. She's been through enough. I know you said you were going to get your son, but this isn't the way to do it."

I leaned back in my chair. "And what, exactly, am I doing?"

Hagen slammed his hands on the desk. "You will not seduce her and then break it off. I know that's your plan. She was eighteen when all of it went down."

"And now she's twenty-eight."

"You're an asshole."

I shrugged. "Why are you involved?"

"Because Amelia is Starlight's best friend. Hurting her will affect Starlight, and I will fucking rearrange your face before I let that happen."

"Speaking of Penny, did you discuss why she helped Amelia keep my son from me?"

I tried not to focus on the fact my own mother had suspected the truth and kept it from me too.

"Do you really think that shit? She's been our number-one defender for years." Hagen shook his head. "It killed her not to say anything. Amelia never outright told Penny. She started suspecting the truth as Christopher grew but saw the life Amelia had with

Stavros and decided to keep her thoughts to herself until six months ago. Amelia and Stavros were good parents to Christopher."

"I would have been a good father to him."

"Come off of your high horse. Back then, all you saw was the next meet, the next record to conquer. You were so self-centered that it shocked everyone that Amelia had the ability to ground your hothead nature.

"A baby would have taken Amelia's attention away from you, and you would have resented having a newborn stifle your life. And believe me, you would have had to make sacrifices you couldn't handle."

It hurt to know Hagen was probably right. I was a self-centered bastard. Being a nineteen-year-old hothead athlete with an eighteen-year-old pregnant girlfriend wouldn't have helped my career. But then again, I'd destroyed my career when I couldn't deal with losing Amelia.

"It would have been my choice. She took that from me."

"I repeat. You're an asshole."

"We established that already."

"This isn't about Christopher at all, is it? It's about your broken fucking heart and making her pay."

I glared at Hagen. The dick was towering over me like I was ten years old and scared shitless of him. Yeah, he could probably kick my ass, but I'd give him a good fight.

"You think you have all the answers. You're wrong. I want to be a part of my child's life."

"Then you better not use his mother."

"I have rights." No one could deny that, but what was the point of rights when I could only pursue them by hurting the very child I wanted?

"Legally you have rights, but remember we lived through what happened when the anger between our parents tainted everything in their children's lives. There are reasons why our lives went the way they did."

I clenched my jaw. That was another thing I avoided thinking about. I hadn't known until recently the reason behind my parents' tumultuous relationship.

My memories of my early childhood were of parents who adored each other. The house was full of laughter and happiness. Then things changed around the time Collin had decided to expand his real-estate business to Las Vegas. He'd organized funding through an investor back in Greece who demanded results, and therefore Collin had to put in long hours, essentially living at work. At the same time, my mother withdrew from him, focusing on her sons and her friends.

Then, when I was a little over ten, my mother up and disappeared for five months, saying she had the opportunity to travel with her friends. It seemed strange at the time. Mama never went anywhere without us in tow. She would call us her loveable luggage.

When she returned, life was completely different. Collin had become an angry man, and the love I'd known between my parents had disappeared. In its place was resentment and bitterness.

It wasn't until a few months ago when I'd had a blow-up with Hagen for rekindling his relationship with Collin that I learned that Mama had cheated on Collin with his best friend, Victor Anthony. An affair that lasted years and led to not only an embezzlement scandal where Collin lost millions, but also the birth of a child who wasn't his.

It had been like a gut punch to learn that Collin was as much a victim of the relationship as Mama. It didn't excuse Collin for all the shit he put my brothers and me through, but it explained a lot.

I still felt like there was more to the story, but Hagen hadn't divulged anything else.

"What aren't you telling me? That Collin was forced to throw each of us out in order to protect our illegitimate baby sister? A sister you haven't seen fit to reveal."

For a brief second, shock passed in Hagen's eyes. "You could say that."

Hagen sat on the chair across from my desk and ran a frustrated hand through his black hair.

"Pour us a drink. This is going to take some time and will add context to Collin's letter and everything that happened with Amelia."

I stood, going to the bar I had in the corner of my office,

poured two tumblers of whiskey, set one in front of Hagen, and braced myself for another bombshell.

"Go on," I pushed.

Hagen threw back the alcohol as if it were water and pulled out his phone, scrolling through his pictures until he landed on one of Penny, Amelia, Henna, and a much younger Anaya.

"One of these girls is our sister."

I knew who it was, immediately. How the hell had I never noticed? She looked like Mama. The same hazel eyes and the Cupid's-bow mouth. It was as if I were seeing a mini version of Mama. The only difference was her caramel-toned skin that she'd inherited from Victor Anthony's Indian heritage.

Swallowing the lump in my throat, I said, "Well, we know Penny and Ame are out. I can see you're into some sick shit, but fucking your sister isn't one of them."

"Asshole."

"Does Penny know?"

"Yes."

Of course, she did. The man kept nothing from her.

"What about Henna?"

"How the fuck do I know? Starlight says Henna has never, ever mentioned it. But I can only assume she does. It would be odd to have your mom be skinny and shaped like a supermodel and then turn up the next month looking the same but with a new baby sister."

"Do you think Anaya knows?"

"I doubt it. From what I've gathered, Anaya has a hatred for her father for all the pain he put her mother through. She is extremely protective of Lena Anthony, to the point of being overbearing. Those are Starlight's words, not mine."

"Are we going to tell Zack?"

Hagen shook his head. "Not yet. He isn't ready. It's going to take him some time to digest the news about Mama. Telling him that Anaya is the product of her cheating isn't going to go down well, especially with this love-hate thing he has going on with her sister."

People thought I was the volatile one of the three brothers, but in truth that was Zack. He was impulsive in a way I could never be, and when pushed he took risks that made me worry for his safety. Hagen may have worked for the mob, but Zack was the guy who would try to *take on* the mob.

"Christ." I ran a hand over my face. "She was in front of us on and off for years. Hell, the number of times she's been at our monthly poker games with Henna. How the hell did we not see it? She has so many of our features."

"I've been asking myself that for months."

"There's more, I can feel it. Collin protected the Anthony women. I want to know why."

"I think you need to bring the whiskey decanter here. It's going to take the whole bottle to get through this."

I got up and grabbed two from the bar in the corner, handed one to Hagen, and then set one in front of me.

"So the story starts and ends with Draco Jackson."

A melia

"Penny, I swear this dress looks like it is going to fall off my body. I'm never letting you or Henna pick another one of my outfits." I double-checked the clip on the back of my neck, holding my halter-style custom-designed Badgley Mischka gown. It was black with a slight shimmer and an open back that went almost to the upper curve of my ass. Then there was the slit that went so high, it made me worry I would expose my goods if I moved wrong.

"Whatever." Penny smoothed her strapless Valentino gown and reached for the purse sitting on the coffee table of her penthouse living room. "I think it looks perfect. Besides, it's not like you have someone who's going to lose his shit that you wore it."

I knew she was referring to the dress Henna and I had picked for the opening of the hotel side of the Ida resort. From what Henna had relayed, Hagen about threw Penny over his shoulder when he saw her wearing the gown that displayed her assets. The magazines had applauded Penny's style as classy yet daring. They also noted the scowl on Hagen's face whenever anyone looked in Penny's direction.

"When I had the gown altered for your short self, you weren't with him." I defended my choice. "If I remember the tabloid pictures, I'm positive the outfit got you thoroughly fucked."

Penny's face flushed, making her green eyes grow brighter. "Yeah, well. This dress may help get you laid tonight."

"Fat chance. Tonight is not about pleasure. It's to focus on all the media and sponsorship bigwigs that will promote the fight."

"From the way it looked the other night, there was a certain promoter who wanted in your pants in an intense way."

Penny mentioning Pierce had my core clenching. Despite all the drama and fallout awaiting me, I couldn't get him, or the memories of everything we'd done together, out of my mind. For the last few days, he'd haunted my dreams and even my waking thoughts.

Going to bed with Pierce was the last thing I planned to do, but fantasizing about him was another matter altogether.

"I won't lie. The attraction is still there."

Penny smirked. "Can we say understatement? I saw the pictures from the club. It's a wonder you two didn't burn the place down."

"What pictures?" I turned to look at her.

"Seriously?" Penny glared at me and walked to the end table in the living room, picked up her phone, and typed in a web address before handing the device to me. "I know you don't share my love of tabloid gossip, but you could at least keep up with the local news."

I studied the screen, and immediately, my stomach dropped. Pierce and I looked like lovers, so into each other that the world had disappeared.

The headline read: "Is History Repeating Itself?"

Fuck. That's what I got for unplugging from all things media for a few days.

I set the phone on the coffee table. "It can't happen, Penny. I have Christopher to think about."

My gaze went to the night sky outside Penny and Hagen's penthouse. The Strip glowed from below, making it seem like we were in another world.

"What better scenario than his parents getting back together?"

I moved to the glass doors of the balcony, setting my hand on the window.

"It wouldn't be like that, and you know it. There's no future for us. Christopher is Stavros's son to the world, and it will stay that way. All I can hope for is an arrangement that will allow Pierce into our lives without diminishing Stavros's legacy."

"Does it matter that you never got over Pierce and the fact you're still in love with each other?" Penny came up behind me.

I shook my head. "He's not in love with me. I killed whatever he felt the day I left him for Stavros."

I could still see the look of utter devastation on his face when I'd told him I was moving and we had no future. He'd listened to my bullshit explanation and hadn't given any response, except the haze of pain that had filled his eyes as he'd turned his back on me and walked away.

I wrapped my arms around myself, trying to ward off the chill that crept through my body.

"I don't believe that for a second. With one touch, you caged the beast Pierce was about to unleash on Henna the other night for suggesting she take you home instead of him. The man hasn't gotten over you."

"Nothing can come of it."

"Well, at least you didn't deny how you felt." Penny laid her head on my shoulder.

"It doesn't matter what I feel. I made decisions that changed the course of our lives. The fact that I forgave Collin doesn't change what I did."

"Are you ever going to forgive yourself for the decision you had to make as a barely eighteen-year-old?"

Before I could respond, the elevator opened and Hagen appeared. "Ready, ladies?"

He offered us his arms, and we left their penthouse.

An hour after arriving at the Cypress, I sipped expensive champagne and watched Apollo charm every reporter and potential sponsor around him. His unique charisma had everyone eating out of his hand.

Apollo caught me watching him and lifted his glass with a grin, and then scowled as he scanned the room before returning to his conversation.

I knew who he was searching for. Neya.

I hadn't figured out what was up with the two of them, since both denied any relationship outside the gym. They had a chemistry that was obvious to everyone around them. If there was a couple who could understand the sacrifice and time needed for an MMA career, it was them. Maybe one day they'd figure it out and...

My thoughts trailed off as I caught sight of Pierce walking in with Hugo and four other fighters of his.

God, he was breathtaking.

He wore a custom-made suit from his go-to designer, Ermenegildo Zegna. Years ago, I learned during a tour of the Zegna studios with Stavros that Pierce, Hagen, and Zack exclusively wore the brand when it came to suits, jackets, and formalwear. One of the designers had said it was rumored the exclusivity clause was due to the fact Zack had lost a hand of poker to one of the heirs of the company. I wasn't sure how much merit there was to the story, but it looked like all of the men with Pierce were wearing the brand, and it was well-placed marketing for the company.

I grabbed another champagne glass from a passing tray and studied Pierce.

He tugged at the knot of his tie, telling me he hated wearing it.

Some things never changed. Even when we were younger, he would avoid a tie if at all possible. He lifted his hand from the silk to shake the hand of a well-known liquor distributor.

I should have looked away, but an image flashed in my mind of him sliding the tie through his fingers and wrapping it around my wrists as he bound me to the headboard of a bed. My blood heated, and arousal hummed deep inside my being.

God, I wanted him, not just for sex but for the edge he would bring me to that bordered on the cusp of pleasure and pain before he would send me over the abyss of ecstasy.

At that moment, he looked up, his heated gaze locked with mine as if he'd read my thoughts, and it took all my strength not to look away.

My pulse thudded in my chest, and desire flooded my core.

What was happening to me? His presence alone had my body responding, and then add in a heated gaze, and I was ready and willing to drop to my knees to suck his cock.

I turned my face to keep myself from acting out my crazy desires.

He was too potent for me to resist him. I was a moth being drawn toward a flame.

Fuck. I wasn't the naive virgin who'd fallen for the bad boy of swimming anymore. I was the promoter who had a thriving business and a son to protect.

"He still wants you," came a heavily Greek-accented voice from behind me.

I froze for a split second.

Why the hell was he here?

I turned to see Astros Dukas, Stavros's best friend, standing before me. He was like an overbearing uncle, the kind who didn't necessarily care about you but cared more about what you could do for him. And the fact he was here in the US had my back up. I never liked him or his wife. I only tolerated them for Stavros's sake, and I knew the feeling was mutual.

"What are you doing here, Astros?"

He set a hand on my back, and I instinctively shifted to the side. His presence always made my skin crawl. It was as if my senses could detect something was off behind the polished, handsome exterior.

"I worried about you and wanted to give you my support."

Everything in me wanted to call bullshit, but I plastered on a smile. Astros thought I hadn't known that he expected Stavros to leave the voting interest in Thanos International to him.

Stavros had told me he'd made the agreement after his first wife, Sara, died from complications during her pregnancy. He'd never expected to marry again or have children, especially after malaria had left him sterile, and most of his other family members were happy living a hands-off life as long as the money came in, so he'd promised Astros his shares in his family's company as an inheritance for Astros's sons.

When he met and married me, he'd assumed Astros understood that our son would inherit the company instead.

I hadn't realized Astros had actually expected Stavros to gift him some of the shares, until the details of Stavros's will and trust were made public. Nothing could make me forget the rage on Astros's face when he learned Christopher would inherit everything with me as the overseer until he came of age.

Astros had always treated me with a distant tolerance, something I assumed had to do with me marrying a man fifteen years older than me and coming from a non-aristocratic background. But until that day, I hadn't noticed the animosity he'd had toward Christopher.

It was as if Astros was angry at Christopher's existence. When he'd looked at my boy, there was pure hatred.

"As you can see, I'm fine. Where's Naomi?" I searched the room for his wife. "I wouldn't think she'd let you leave Europe without her."

Everyone assumed I was a gold-digger when in fact she was. I'd never met a person that enjoyed the finer things in life more than her. Astros was her meal ticket. Which meant she had to do everything to keep him interested, from having lots of children and keeping her figure perfect, to turning the other way when Astros flaunted his many affairs.

It still boggled my mind how Stavros and Astros were so completely different.

"She is on a trip with her friends. In Fiji, I believe."

I folded my arms. "Why are you really here?"

"I had business in California and decided to stop by to see you."

It took all my strength not to roll my eyes and mutter, "Or maybe you wanted to get my position on the sale of the Singapore shipyard."

Instead, I plastered on a fake smile and said, "George

has my vote in a sealed envelope. He'll announce it at the board meeting."

After Stavros's death, I knew I had no clue what it was like to run a shipping conglomerate, so I'd let Stavros's executive vice president and nephew, Lucas Thanos, take the reins as President and CEO of Thanos International. I remained Chairman of the Board and made the final decisions on major acquisitions and changes. But the day-to-day workings of the company were Lucas's to handle. This also gave me time to run my own management and promotion company.

"I see." He gave me a disingenuous smile. "You know what's best for Christopher's future."

"I try. I need to make the rounds. I'll see you back home in a few months."

He caught my arm. "Why don't you introduce me to everyone. We could make it a fun evening."

I gently but firmly pulled free of Astros's hold. "Tonight is business, Astros. That means making sure everything is ready for the fight while helping Apollo further his career. I'm not here for a social event."

"Well, Lykaios definitely pulled out the red carpet for you tonight."

"Not for me. It's for Apollo," I corrected. "This is a way for the press to get to know the fighters better before they go into seclusion for their training."

"Right. And it has nothing to do with Collin Lykaios

adopting you into his fold as he's done with the Anthony girls." There was a hint of distaste in his words that had my temper rising. "He should be careful with the people linked to his name."

"Henna and Anaya had nothing to do with their father's deeds. Lay off them. They're my friends." I couldn't hide the irritation in my voice.

Astros lifted his hands in surrender. "I'm only watching out for you and Christopher, as Stavros would expect me to. I don't want anything negative to touch either of you."

His words only annoyed me further.

"I'm a smart woman and know who to trust."

"You know Naomi and I will always be there for you." He leaned down to kiss my cheek, lingering longer than necessary.

"Goodbye, Astros."

He nodded and moved out of the ballroom area. When I turned to find Apollo, I saw Pierce scowling at me with anger in his gaze.

CHAPTER EIGHT

PIERCE

Who the fuck was she talking to? Another older lover? Of course with that thing she called a dress on, every man in the room had fantasies of getting between her legs.

I ran a hand through my hair, squeezing my nape.

Dammit. She wasn't mine. I hadn't felt this sense of jealousy since we were kids. Then she was my safe place, the one person who was mine. I had no say in what she did today.

Collin saw my reaction and smirked, making me want to strangle the man who'd provided my DNA. I couldn't reconcile everything Hagen told me and what Collin had written in the letter with the man who'd thrown my brothers and me out of his home as children.

Hagen had given me the background of the whole Draco-Collin saga, but that meant shit to my world as it existed. Because of him, my last memories of my mother were of her ravaged by cancer in the hospital. Because of him, I lost the woman I loved and a chance to be a father. It would take a whole lot more than a letter and apology.

Collin turned as Amelia approached him. He hugged her as if she were his long-lost daughter before she moved into the crowd with Apollo. What had he said to earn her forgiveness?

I clenched my fists and then adjusted my tie. I needed to burn off this frustration with Collin, Amelia, the whole damn situation. After this shindig, I planned to head to my place and hit the pool.

Hagen would probably bitch, but I was miserable company, and it was better for me to swim than brood while sitting in one of his clubs.

Amelia glanced in my direction for a brief moment, and immediately I felt the deep pull we'd barely touched on the other night. I craved her, not just physically but the bond we'd shared, a bond that could never be rekindled.

"Looks like you're staking a claim." Hugo came up next to me and clasped a palm on my back, jostling me a fraction.

Man, the fucker had a powerful hand. Hopefully, he'd remember to use it in the ring.

"So what's the deal with the two of you? Rumor has it she left you for some billionaire."

"You could say that."

I watched her move fluidly between the various media representatives. She gave them smiles and flirted while keeping Apollo the center of the conversation. Anyone who encountered her would never doubt that she knew her job.

She'd grown into a honed businesswoman. Gone was the innocent, shy girl who'd turned my world upside down with a glance. Gone was the girl who had a hard time speaking in public. And most definitely, gone was the girl who needed me as much as I'd needed her.

"So want to tell me if something is going on with you two?"

I frowned. "Why is that any of your business?"

"Because I need to know that whatever it is, it won't affect my career. Remember we talked about me taking on some matches in Europe and Asia. If you have a falling out, it'll make it harder to get prime spots."

"I hear you." I continued to watch Amelia. "We have some things from the past to resolve. It'll be done in private. Neither Amelia nor I would do anything to hurt our people."

"Good to hear. Now I have another prospect to discuss."

I smiled. Hugo was young but had a good head on his shoulders, especially when it came to his future.

As he began to go into details, Amelia glanced around the room, focusing on a door in the back. She moved toward it, stopping to greet people and engage in small talk. It took her about ten minutes to work her way back and slip out.

"I see that I'm boring you." Hugo smacked my back again. "I may be young, but I'm not blind. You have it bad for her."

"You need your eyes checked."

"Says the man who's itching to go after her."

⸻

Amelia

I stepped into the lounge Collin said he used for his VIPs. He'd kept it closed for me, and I was eternally grateful. I'd escaped to this room countless times over the past few days. I was a shy person by nature, but my lifestyle and business had made it necessary to pretend I was an extrovert. Sometimes I wondered how people hadn't caught on to my anxiety. Collin knew my stage-fright issues from the time my father had worked for him, so I found it sweet that he cared enough to give me a space to collect my thoughts, whenever I needed it.

I moved to the stocked bar near the doors leading to the lounge's balcony and poured a large helping of Firewater, downing it almost immediately. I winced as the whiskey burned down my throat and then warmed my belly.

How did Penny go shot for shot with this stuff and still have her wits? Another one of these and I'd be out for the night, in dreamland.

Once the sting eased, I set my glass down and gazed out of the large windows that looked out toward a slew of dancing water fountains.

I pressed my palm to the glass and sighed. I was playing a dangerous game with Pierce. One that guaranteed I'd be the one who came out the loser. We had a child we hadn't yet discussed and an attraction that I couldn't act upon.

Then there was the added worry I felt at seeing Astros here. If he learned that Stavros wasn't Christopher's father, he'd do everything in his power to embarrass the Thanos family and put a taint on me and Christopher. He was dangerous, and I had to keep an eye on him.

The years I'd spent by Stavros's side had taught me more than I ever expected. He'd shown me how to gauge people, their motives especially. I learned what was shown wasn't truth. Countless times, people had smiled to my face but treated me as less than an equal when the press or the public wasn't watching. Astros and his wife were the biggest culprits of this.

There was only one reason Astros was here. He had to have seen the pictures of Pierce and me. From what I saw at Penny and Hagen's place, those pictures would leave no doubt our attraction was as strong today as it had been.

I pushed the thought back as a door opened behind me. Immediately, the energy changed in the room, and I knew it was Pierce before I turned.

"What are you doing in—" My words were lost as I took in the feral lust in his gaze. He stalked toward me and jerked me into his arms a second before his mouth descended on mine.

Need I'd tried so hard to push back erupted in every pore of my body. He tasted of champagne and his unique rich flavor that I could never forget.

I gripped his shoulders, knowing I should push him away. Instead I pulled him closer.

"Do you know how hard it is to see men want you and not have any claim to stop them? This fucking dress is indecent." He bit my lower lip, leaving a delicious sting.

"I wear what I want. I'm a grown woman," I said between kisses.

He cupped my ass, grinding my pelvis along his. His hold was hard and possessive as if he owned me.

"Believe me, I know."

His tongue pushed into my mouth as his grip on my bottom grew more intense. His fingers branded my skin under the dress. I nearly came.

God, it had been so long. I thought this need for domination was dead.

I was wrong. So wrong.

My hands slid into his hair, gripping it tight as he deepened the kiss.

He pushed aside the thigh slit of my gown and gripped my hips, lifting me against him. Instinctively I wrapped my legs around his waist while continuing to feast on his lips.

I let out a surprised gasp as my back hit the sofa.

"Pierce, what are you doing?" I asked against his mouth, a little too breathlessly.

"I thought it was obvious." He stared down at me. "All I've wanted since we danced at the club was to touch every inch of your body. With my lips, my hands, my cock."

There was a lingering thought in the back of my mind someone could walk in, but I pushed it away. My breasts were heavy and achy, feeling constricted by my dress. Pierce cupped them as if he'd read my mind. He kneaded them with firm, demanding squeezes.

I wanted more.

One of his hands slid to the back of my neck, and the next thing I knew, he'd unfastened the halter strap of my gown.

He broke our kiss to trail his tongue down my throat and over my collarbone.

"Pierce," I moaned, arching into his touch.

He pushed my dress down, exposing my breasts before latching on to one straining nipple while rolling and tugging on the other with his fingers. He wasn't gentle. There was a bite to his ministrations. He nipped and sucked as he sent shock waves of pain and pleasure into my body. My pussy wept and spasmed with each pull of his mouth. He tormented both tips until I was writhing under him.

"I need more." His voice was thick with desire.

He bunched my dress upward, settling his body between my thighs. He rubbed his straining erection against my clitoral nub. I squirmed to get away and at the same time wrapped my leg tighter around him.

"I have to see you come." Pierce gazed down at me. "I will see you come."

He didn't give me a chance to respond and covered my lips with his. We continued to eat at each other as his fingers slipped past the gusset of my underwear and to my soaked core. He stroked up and down my damp cleft, spreading my juices over my sex, and then pushed a finger inside, curving it upward to graze the sensitive area of nerves hidden at the top. His thumb glided up and teased my throbbing clit.

My back bowed as my pussy flooded with my arousal, soaking his hand.

"That's it," he murmured as he bit down on the juncture of my neck and shoulder. "Let's see if this still makes you go over."

Another finger joined the first and then a third, adding a bit of the discomfort I craved.

He began to thrust, setting a pace that was rough and measured. My core quickened, and before I realized what was happening, I slid over the cliff of ecstasy. My body thrashed as my pussy clamped down on his pistoning fingers.

"Pierce. Oh God. Pierce," I cried out while digging my nails into his back.

He kept the pace of his hand until he wrung out every drop of my release and I was limp underneath him.

He pulled free of my body and held my gaze as he licked my essence from his fingers. There was raging desire burning in his eyes, reigniting the trembling of my pussy.

Sliding my hand between us, I cupped his straining cock. I circled his bulging head before I squeezed his hard girth. He was thick and long, just as I remembered.

I'd thought he'd torn me in half the first time we'd made love. We'd been so frenzied to get it on that we'd skipped foreplay so I could accommodate his size and jumped to penetration. We'd both been virgins then, not having any clue what to do besides the mechanics of the act.

Pierce was no longer an inexperienced man. He knew what he was doing and how to ready my body.

A stab of jealousy hit me as I envisioned all the women he'd been with over the years. I knew it wasn't fair or rational, but I couldn't help it.

Pierce cupped my chin and peered down at me. "I'm going to fuck you now. I would have preferred for our first time again to be in a bed, but this will have to do."

I jerked my face free as some semblance of sanity returned.

"We can't do this. It'll complicate things. I already let it go too far."

He gripped my wrists and pinned them above my head as he looked over me.

My heart pounded into my head, and the feel of his hard grip opened another lock on a desire I shouldn't explore.

"No, it'll uncomplicate it. This sexual tension between us is too distracting. I know you're going back to Greece, so there won't be any expectations. We fuck, you submit, and we get each other out of our systems. Then we return to our lives."

His words were like a bucket of cold water thrown on me.

I jerked out of his hold and pushed him back. "No. I can't do this. I don't do casual sex."

I tugged on my dress, and with unsteady fingers, I refastened the strap around my neck. Then I rested my arms on my knees while covering my face with my hands.

My body ached for him, both physically and emotionally. I took a few deep breaths while trying to hold in the sobs of frustration and need.

I lifted my face to see the hard expression on his.

"Bullshit. You were fucking Thanos while we were together."

I held his stare but kept quiet, suppressing the urge to defend myself.

He would learn the truth soon enough. What just happened now made it clear it was imperative I talk to Pierce about Christopher.

Breaking eye contact, I slipped off the sofa and straightened my clothes.

"You shouldn't have come in here. I shouldn't have let it get this far. It was a mistake. I'm sorry."

I rushed to the door, but as I grabbed the door handle, Pierce asked, "Did you ever love me or was it only one-sided?"

Without thinking I answered, "I loved you so much that it destroyed me to break your heart. You can hate me all you want, but circumstances made hurting you the only choice."

"Like being knocked up and marrying another man."

I flinched and my voice grew hard as I said, "That is something we will discuss at another time."

"When is the right time? I have a right to know what happened."

"Tomorrow," I said, knowing it was time and there was no way of getting out of it. "Meet me here at two. I have training sessions to oversee until one."

"No, meet me at my hotel. I don't want anything or anyone distracting us."

"Fine." I tugged the door open.

Just as I crossed the threshold, Piece said, "I'm going to fuck you, Ame. Make you beg and feed every craving you try so hard to hide. It's inevitable. I'd rather it be with everything laid out on the table."

CHAPTER NINE

"Mr. Lykaios, I have Mrs. Thanos seated at the corner table as you requested."

I nodded at Nico Maxim, the manager of Marmara, the three-star Michelin restaurant in the Aegean.

"I'll show myself in. Make sure you keep this section closed."

"Yes, sir."

As I worked my way around a slate and multicolored pebble waterfall wall, I noticed a group of diners who looked eerily similar to Draco Jackson's men.

From the way they watched me and then glanced in the direction I was heading, they were keeping an eye on what went on in my world. A world that had no ties to Draco's.

I had to remember to ask Hagen about it. Right now, I had to focus on the woman waiting for me.

I came around the corner from where she sat and stopped to study her.

God, she was beautiful. She wore a light dusting of makeup, and her black hair was loose. Her pink-and-black suit with an open collar gave the perfect hint of sexiness without looking trashy. This wasn't the fighter I'd fallen for but the savvy businesswoman with a reputation for playing hardball.

She scrolled through her phone as she sipped her drink, probably sparkling water. She'd been addicted to the stuff when we were kids. She licked her lips, and I nearly groaned.

I could still taste her on my tongue. Watching her go over was like falling into the past. The right touch and she'd surrendered all her control.

We'd been so naive when we played as barely grown teens. Neither of us understood the dynamics between us.

She was so controlled in the outside world, knowing one wrong move could cost her a match, or worse, a dangerous injury. I, on the other hand, had no control of my world. The only thing I was good at was swimming, and even then I had to learn to handle the disorder of my family life, a mother and baby brother I wasn't allowed to contact, a father who tried to control my life but had thrown me out the second I'd turned eighteen, and a career that demanded so much of my time that without Hagen to guide me I'd never have been able to handle it.

It wasn't until Amelia and I started seeing each other that I lost my reputation as a reckless, combative teen who would challenge anyone who told me no.

She'd given me a way to handle my chaotic life.

Almost a decade later, I clearly understood we'd played in something neither of us had any business exploring. We were too young, too ignorant of the do's and don'ts, too unaware of the dangers. I cringed thinking of the lines I thankfully never crossed but no doubt would have if Amelia and I had stayed together.

It had taken me years of training to hone the desires that came naturally to me. When I took Amelia again, she would have a very different experience.

As if she felt my gaze, she looked up from her phone. She swallowed, and a shadow of wariness entered her eyes.

Slowly approaching, I let her take me in. There was always a slight change in her breath whenever I neared her. She more than likely wasn't even aware of it.

"Sorry for keeping you waiting, Ame," I said, grazing a finger behind her neck and then moving to the seat opposite her at the table.

She shivered and clenched her glass, making me almost smile.

"It's fine. I ordered you a whiskey."

I glanced at the tumbler of amber liquid on my side. She'd noticed what I liked within the few interactions we'd had.

Why did the thought of that please me?

Snap out of it, man. You're not a lovestruck teen anymore.

I picked up the glass and took a sip before setting it back on the table. I remained quiet as she rubbed her fingers along the stem of her glass.

"Pierce," she began, "I need you to listen without interrupting me. Once I'm done, I'll answer any questions you have." Her hands shook as she tucked her hair behind her ear.

"Okay."

"When I left you, there were more things at play than you knew. Hell, more than I knew. Some of it I haven't learned about until recently. I always assumed Collin hated us together because I wasn't good enough for you. And threatened to fire my father to break us up."

"It did break us up."

"No. There was more to it."

Okay, that sounded ominous. I leaned forward. "Go on."

"I'm going to tell you a story. There was an heiress named Rhea who fell for Collin, an older businessman. Their romance was a whirlwind, passionate and intense. It was perfect for years. They had three children. Sons. These boys were their world."

Her painting my parents in a storybook romance had my back up. I opened my mouth to ask what this had to do with my son, but she lifted her hand.

"Please, Pierce. Let me finish, and you will understand."

I nodded.

"A year after their youngest child was born, the couple moved to Las Vegas with their children. Collin wanted to create a legacy for his family, so he began to work nonstop, not realizing he was neglecting the very people he worked so hard for. The relationship between Rhea and Collin became strained, and Rhea turned to Collin's best friend for comfort."

"Anthony," I said without thinking.

She didn't acknowledge my words. "Then one day, Collin's offices were raided by federal agents, looking for evidence against—" she paused before continuing, "—Anthony. It turned out Collin was one of many victims of an embezzlement scandal. An investigation revealed that Anthony had seduced Rhea to gain access to Collin's financials.

"Reeling from the discovery, Collin confronted Rhea. She admitted the truth and begged him for forgiveness. They tried to fix their marriage for their sons' sakes, but a month later she discovered she was pregnant with

Anthony's child. A child she gave up after a secret birth. A child I didn't discover was a friend of mine for most of my life until a conversation I had with my mother."

Holy fuck. She knew Anaya was my sister.

"The reason Collin wanted us apart was that he was afraid your mother's secret would be exposed if we stayed together. My parents were the ones who arranged for your mother to deliver without anyone suspecting.

"At the time, my father worked for one of Collin's resorts near Athens and wanted desperately to move to America. Knowing this, Collin made a deal with him. In exchange for hiding Rhea in Greece for the duration of her pregnancy, Collin would sponsor work visas for my parents and a green card for me, give Papa a job as a gaming manager in one of his casinos, and pay for my education. And once the baby was born, my parents would arrange for Anthony's wife to take the little girl.

"Once we moved to Las Vegas, Rhea maintained a friendly but distant relationship with my parents. Collin was formal and all business, although he had helped me with the application process for my American citizenship.

"For years, Collin and Rhea's secret was well maintained.

"It wasn't until they learned you and I were in a relationship that everything changed. They feared our involvement would cause my parents to slip and reveal their secrets and..."

"And they forced you to break up with me. I know what happened ten years ago. What's the point of this long story?" I couldn't hide the hard edge in my voice. "Except to waste my time."

It killed me inside to see my mother as anything other than the amazing woman who adored her children. She'd cheated on Collin, and because of her affair with Anthony, Draco had orchestrated the destruction of my childhood.

I pushed the hurt down. I couldn't go there right now.

"Because you needed to know Collin's reasoning for pushing me to my decision and why I forgave him."

I slammed a fist on the table, making her jump. I was done with the pretense.

"A decision that had me losing nearly ten years of my son's life."

I pulled out a set of pictures from my jacket and threw them on the table.

I positioned two of them side-by-side. "You see this picture? This is me. And this one is Christopher Thanos. We look identical. Tell me he's not mine. I dare you."

"I...I can't," she stuttered, and then after a deep breath, she said, "He's yours."

"Did you know you were carrying my child when you broke up with me?"

A tear slipped down her cheek. "I didn't know until three weeks later."

"You didn't think it was important to let me know?"

"I did. I was going to come to your apartment and lay out everything that happened, but you'd moved on. A tabloid had caught you in a hotel with two models."

I ran a hand through my hair. "What did you expect me to do? You ripped my heart out of my chest."

I was fucking nineteen with women throwing themselves at me. I had to forget Amelia and I had taken what was offered. The fact I felt dirty and disgusted with myself afterward was another matter altogether.

"Not jump into bed with anything that would spread her legs," she said through clenched teeth.

"And when was the first time you slept with your billionaire?"

"Six months after I had Christopher." Her eyes blazed. "You see, I was in love with your pompous ass and couldn't imagine touching another man, whether we were together or not. Something you had no problem with."

All my anger disappeared. "I still had a right to know."

"Were you really going to be able to step up? You had just won six medals and had a long career ahead of you. The only thing that grounded you was swimming."

She was the only thing that grounded me. When I'd lost her, I lost the ability to control my rage, resulting in a fight with an official and disqualification from the sport for three years. In the sporting world that had been a death sentence.

"It wasn't your decision."

"I can't change the past. All I can say was that I was a scared, pregnant eighteen-year-old. My parents had lost their jobs with no choice but to return to Greece. We had no money, and a good man offered to accept my unborn child and me."

"Why? No one does that. What did he get out of it?"

She looked away again, closing her eyes for a brief second. "He got Christopher. Stavros couldn't have children."

"So you're telling me my son is the heir to a shipping fortune."

"Legally, he is Stavros's son."

"Bullshit. No court in America will agree to that."

"He's not American. He's Greek."

"Wrong. Both his parents are Americans. Therefore he's American."

"As far as the world knows, he's only half American."

I clenched my jaw. "Is it about the money? Are you afraid Christopher will lose his inheritance?"

"No. Stavros made sure nothing in his will or the company bylaws could contest Christopher's claim to the company."

"You sold my child."

"It wasn't like that, and I won't let you taint Stavros's memory with your anger. Stavros loved Christopher more than anything."

"I have rights, Amelia."

"Are you going to fight me for him?" I could feel the fear radiating from her body.

I wanted to scream at her "yes" but instead I said, "Only if you keep me from him."

"I won't prevent you from getting to know Christopher or being in his life, but for now, he will only know Stavros as his father. He's too young to understand what happened between us."

The determination on her face made me want to shake her. I was his father. I had a right to give my son a life I'd never had.

"Then who will I be to him?"

She pinched the bridge of her nose. "I don't know." Then her gaze locked with mine. "How did you find out? Was it Penny or the magazine?"

"Not Penny." I laughed, unable to hide the bitterness I felt toward my soon-to-be sister-in-law. "That woman is loyal to you through and through. Just so you know, Hagen confronted her about it once we learned about Christopher's parentage."

"Then you saw the magazine. That was the only way."

"You're both right and wrong."

"I don't understand."

"The man who's become your best friend sent me an advance copy of *Vogue*. He feels guilty for the fact his grandson lives on a different continent because of his manipulation."

She remained quiet, as if processing what I said.

"Are you surprised?"

"Honestly, no." She sighed and shook her head. "Collin is on a mission to fix the mistakes of the past. It makes me sad to see the guilt he carries on his shoulders."

Her face grew sad for a second.

What had Collin said to get her to forgive him and make her genuinely care for him so much?

"What I don't understand is why he decided to tell you before letting me know? As far as anyone knows, none of his sons are on speaking terms with him."

"He thinks we're going to be one happy family."

"That's impossible. Christopher and I live in Greece. At the end of the summer, we'll go back."

That was just a few months from now.

"Then what do you suggest?"

"Why don't you tell me? You had to have had a plan. Was pretending to want me part of the plan to get my defenses down?"

"The attraction between us is authentic. I don't need to feign interest."

"Then what do you want?"

"What do you think the price of my silence should be? After all, you're the one telling me I can never claim my own child, a child you stole and gave to another man."

"I don't know," she said warily.

Well, fuck. Until this moment, I hadn't thought of

anything but getting in Amelia's face and confronting her about Christopher. It was what had driven me since I learned the truth about the past. Now here she was, ready to do anything for my silence, and I had no idea what to say.

Who the hell was I? I'd never had a hard time knowing what I had to do.

We both remained quiet for a few minutes, staring at each other. Then a thought came to me.

"I want you as my submissive. I want you to surrender all that tightly held control. I want to fuck you every night for the foreseeable future."

She swallowed as a flush crept up her cheeks, and her eyes dilated.

"I told you I don't do casual sex. I've only been with two men in my life."

"It won't be casual. There's more." I paused, knowing I was going to hell for what I was about to say. "We're already tied through Christopher for the rest of our lives. One more connection shouldn't matter."

"I'm not following."

"In compensation for giving my son to another man and my silence, I want a child of my own."

"You can't be serious."

"Dead serious."

Anger flared in her eyes, as did hurt. "I will never have a child just to give him or her up. This discussion is over."

She shifted to leave, but I stopped her with a hand on her arm.

"I never said you would have to give our child up."

"Then what, Pierce? I might even consider sleeping with you again, but a child is off the table."

"How about this? If by the end of the summer you aren't pregnant then we go our separate ways. The only price I will ask for my silence is that I be part of Christopher's life in some capacity."

"But if I am pregnant?"

I was definitely going to hell.

"Then you marry me."

CHAPTER TEN

Amelia

"Penny, we need to talk," I said the second I pulled open the doors to Penny's Firewater lab situated in a set of warehouses on the outskirts of Vegas. It was past work hours, so I knew she'd be holed up in here alone until Hagen carted her home.

On a typical day, I'd be excited to get a peek of her newly renovated and super-high-tech place where she'd created her hundred-million-dollar whiskey empire. But I was too damned pissed off at Pierce, Collin, and her to care.

She was sitting in the corner looking into a microscope with protection goggles on her face.

"I can't believe you didn't let me know that Pierce

knew about Christopher. You're supposed to be my best friend. Why would you keep something so important from me?"

Penny rolled back from her workstation and gave me a worried look. Yeah, she should be scared.

"I wanted to tell you, but Hagen said it was something you had to work out with Pierce."

Her lab coat was stained with amber and brown spots, and her hair was tied in a messy bun atop her head. She was gorgeous with her mixed Greek and Indian heritage. Only she could look stylish while the rest of us would look like a rumpled hot mess in the same attire.

"Oh yeah. We're working it out, all right. That man is insane! It's a wonder I didn't punch him in the face. And believe me, if I had, his nose would be broken right now."

My temper hadn't calmed since I walked out of the meeting with Pierce. The only satisfaction I could get was the shock on his face when I told him to shove his proposal up his ass and that I'd rather see him in court. Maybe I shouldn't have added the last part, but he couldn't expect me to have another child with him, much less marry him.

"Did he propose the joint custody option Hagen and Zack had drawn up?"

Well, it looked like my best friend knew even more than I thought.

"Not even close. For his silence about Christopher's parentage, he wants me to fuck him until the end of the summer. And then, if I'm pregnant, I'm supposed to marry him, with the option to spend half the year in Las Vegas and the other half running my business in Greece."

"You're kidding." She stood and began to pace.

I cocked one hand on my hip and pointed to myself with the other. "Does this look like the face of someone who is kidding?"

She lifted a brow. "Well, it's not like you don't want to sleep with him."

"Don't even joke. I'm so mad at you right now. You broke girl code. And on top of everything else, Collin was the mastermind behind Pierce learning about Christopher."

She winced, telling me she knew all the details.

"What did you say to Pierce?"

I glared at her as if she was stupid. "I am not sleeping with him or having another child with him."

I plopped down on a vacant chair near a bank of beakers, folding my arms across my body.

"I doubt sleeping is what he wants to do with you. From what I hear, he's into the kink side of things. Hell, he owns private clubs in all of the HPZ properties."

A surge of jealousy coursed through me. I'd heard the rumors and knew firsthand where Pierce's tastes lay. I also understood how BDSM clubs worked. One didn't need to be in a committed partnership to engage in scenes. All that was required was consent and safe sex.

"If he can get his rocks off with a submissive any time he wants, why does he want me?"

Penny walked up to me and leaned down, resting a hand on the armrests of my chair. She almost looked like a disappointed teacher about to give me a lecture.

Why was she glaring at me when I was the one who should be pissed off at her?

"Just because he owns them doesn't mean he participates often. From what Hagen said, ever since the negotiations started for the Regalia-Davis fight, he's only visited the clubs for business purposes."

"I doubt Pierce is going to tell his brothers every time he gets laid. I've seen the tabloid pictures. He's never short on companions."

"He may not share the details, but he isn't a guy for casual sex. His last girlfriend was over six months ago. He hasn't been seen with anyone since then. He is a relationship kind of guy and monogamous to the core. The volatile, fly-by-the-seat-of-his-pants, asshole image he has going is just that, an image, not the truth."

Her words felt like a direct hit to the heart. He'd spent the last ten years thinking I cheated on him. Even the world thought I cheated on him with Stavros.

"Then why does he want me? I destroyed his heart."

She sat down heavily and frowned. "You really have no clue, do you?"

"No, I don't. Why don't you tell me, my genius, analytical, scientist friend?"

"Amelia. You are so hard headed. The only reason a man wants to impregnate a woman so he can force her into marrying him is because he is still in love with her. The keeping his silence part is just his way of protecting himself."

I'd have laughed at how crazy her words sounded, if it didn't make me long for it to be true. But I knew otherwise.

"He's not in love with me. He wants me in his bed—it's the price for keeping my secret."

"This is a win-win."

"I can't believe you're saying this to me. I'm not opening that Pandora's box. I can see disaster written all over it and I'll be the one left hurt."

"That's true. You'll be fucked not only literally but also emotionally and mentally."

"Thanks for rephrasing what I said so eloquently, Miss Smartypants."

She stuck her tongue out, reminding me of how thankful I was for the friendship that was unconditional and had survived two decades and a continent apart. And just like that, my temper had calmed—well, with her anyway. I could never stay mad at her, no matter how hard I tried.

We'd been all of eight years old when we'd first met. She was the mousy yet feisty horticulture export-import heiress and me the new girl in school with a thick Greek accent. Penny had come to my defense and punched a boy twice her size when he made fun of me for "talking weird." From that day, we were thick as thieves and more like sisters than friends.

"So are you still mad at me?"

I pursed my lips and muttered, "Yes."

"Liar." She laughed. "So are you going to let him know that you can't have any more children?"

During Christopher's birth, I'd had major complications that resulted in a lot of scarring. The doctors pretty much told me the chances of me carrying another child were slim to none.

Knowing Christopher wouldn't have siblings broke my heart. I'd grown up an only child and always wished for a sister or brother. Stavros had suggested getting a surrogate who would carry my egg and a donor sperm, but we'd decided against it. The fallout would be too high, especially if the media got wind of it.

"No, because I'm not sleeping with Pierce now or ever again."

She coughed "bullshit" and then gave me an innocent smile.

"You're such an ass. It's going to take me a long time to get over your treachery. And no, I don't want a bottle of your secret reserve whiskey. I can barely drink two shots without it going to my head."

I was a flyweight on a good day. Probably because it was frowned upon for any Thanos to be caught with a drink in their hand. We had to set an example, or so my deceased mother-in-law had drilled into my head.

"There has to be a way I can make it up to you."

"Let me think." I tapped my lips. "I know. Tell me more about these clubs in the hotels. They have to be secret, since I doubt any of the brothers would want the public to know they have a kink club on any of their premises, much less all of them."

"I knew it. Behind that all-business, conservative façade, you're a freak who likes to be spanked, tied up, and fucked."

"You read way too many romance novels."

She snorted. "You're one to talk. Who gave me my first kissing book?"

"Whatever. So are you going to tell me about them or not?"

"Why not?"

· ───────

A little after ten in the evening, I walked into the Ida. I tightened the belt of my long, lightweight, black coat and made my way through the casino, following the directions Penny had given me to the Diávolos Lounge.

When I'd grilled Penny on the clubs, I had no

intention of visiting any of them, but then as she described Diávolos, she made it sound like no club I'd ever been to before. Kink clubs weren't something new to me—I'd visited plenty—but this was my chance to see what one designed by Pierce looked like. And so I'd convinced Penny to arrange for admission to the secret club.

I worked my way around a crowd that was admiring the flowers outside of the botanical garden. And then up a set of stairs. This resort always took my breath away. I loved the unique mix of ultra-modern straight lines and fixtures with splashes of vibrant color.

When I came to the place Penny said was the club, I didn't see any indication of a lounge anywhere. That was when I noticed a bouncer in a tailored suit with his arms crossed, standing in a corner.

I walked up to him and said the password Penny said members used to enter the club, "*apagorevménos,*" meaning forbidden.

The bouncer studied me for a moment, then nodded, letting me pass by pushing a wall that opened into a dimly lit hallway. A distant echo of music gave the invitation to enter the main lounge.

I slid a black lace mask over my face and worked my way toward the sound, coming to a reception room with a hostess.

She was a beautiful brunette with blond highlights in various shades. Her deep almond skin and hazel eyes gave away her Middle Eastern heritage. She was petite, dressed in a black silk minidress.

"Hello. I'm Bridgett. Are you a new member?"

"No. I'm a guest for the night." I passed her a card. It was another gift from Penny. With it, I could enjoy the club at my leisure. Or that was what she'd told me when she'd given it to me.

"Please review the club rules and sign in," Bridgett instructed, pushing a folder in my direction.

I quickly read the documents and scrolled my signature. They were standard protocols about consent, safety, and protection.

Bridgett gestured to a man I hadn't noticed standing in the corner.

"José will take your coat. When you're ready to leave, he'll retrieve it for you."

I slipped off my coat and felt the cool air hit my skin. I'd chosen to wear a two-piece black-and-ivory corset ensemble of lace and satin with black thigh highs and heels.

Bridgett set a laminated paper on top of the counter next to a basket that held bracelets in various sizes and colors.

"Here is a list of what each band means. Always know you never have to participate unless you desire. But the bands make it easier for the guests to decipher your preference."

I looked over the band descriptions. Black meant heterosexual, attached dominant; and purple with a black line in the middle meant bisexual, unattached submissive; and everything in between.

I picked a pink with a red line in the middle, stating to anyone who saw it that I was a submissive observer. It allowed me to play voyeur and made it clear to any Dominant interested in me that I wasn't available.

During my various travels, I'd explored a few of the clubs throughout Europe, always as an observer, never a participant, and always anonymous. There was something about the environment that called to me. Stavros had joined me a few times, but I'd known it wasn't his thing and he'd stopped going with me altogether a few years before he passed away.

"You're all set. Follow the path behind the curtain. Enjoy your evening."

"Thank you."

I made my way to a room filled with couples and groups enjoying cocktails and food. It had a jazz-lounge atmosphere. Most of the clubs I'd visited had a common area where patrons could socialize. The only difference between normal clubs and this one was the attire of the guests—from gowns to barely-there lingerie for the women, and three-piece suits to speedos for the men. The states of dress and undress represented their status, submissive or Dom.

The sense of hedonism in the air made my skin prickle with awareness. An attractive Latino man in fitted jeans and a black T-shirt scanned me from head to toe and back, lingering on my wristband. My body instinctively reacted.

Definitely a Dom. His band was black with a thin white line going down the center, telling me he was a heterosexual, unattached Dominant.

What would it be like to participate, just once? I shook the thought away. Fantasizing about it was one thing, but doing it was another. I wasn't into casual sex. Sex meant too much to me.

I noticed a group going up a set of stairs and decided to follow. The second I reached the landing, I saw the unique setup of the public playrooms giving the illusion of privacy, with the exception of the tables and chairs placed for optimal viewing of the action in the rooms.

I licked my dry lips and moved to observe one of the rooms. Three couples were engaged in hard sex, oblivious to anything but the people in the scene with them. Every few minutes they switched partners.

That was definitely not my thing. I moved to another room and was immediately mesmerized. A beautiful blond woman was bound to a St. Andrew's Cross while her Dom circled her. He stroked her with every pass, touching her breasts, stomach, thighs, face, or legs, but never touching the one place she wanted him to. She writhed against the cross, moaning at the displeasure of being denied. He murmured words of love and affection with a little sweet teasing. They both wore wristbands in addition to wedding rings, telling me they were a committed couple. The Dom stopped touching his submissive, moving to the back of the room and picking up a soft-tailed bullwhip. My breath hitched as he snapped the leather over and over, not touching his submissive but making it very clear to her that he would caress her with the sting of it.

My nipples hardened as I thought about what it would feel like to have a whip heat my skin. Arousal throbbed a slow, steady beat between my legs, almost matching the music playing over the speakers. I wanted to press my thighs together but stayed still.

When the Dom landed the first strike, I couldn't help but gasp as if I were the one struck, as if Pierce were the one doing it. I wanted so desperately to feel the pleasurable pain of the whip's bite. To have it bring me to the cusp of orgasm until one strategic flick of a wrist had me going over.

I watched, enthralled as the Dom did exactly as I fantasized about. By the time the scene ended and the Dom darkened the glass observation windows, I was hot, aroused, and dripping with sweat. Added to it was the fact I was annoyed with myself for imagining Pierce as the man wielding the whip.

Never had a scene affected me this way. I closed my eyes for a brief second and released a deep breath.

"Wow," I whispered.

"Are you sure you only want to observe?" came a deep voice next to my ear. "I could make it well worth your while to play."

I turned to find the man who'd checked me out in the lounge.

"I'm only here to observe. I don't ever participate."

"That's too bad." There was a tinge of humor in his words. "I'm Ronaldo." He took my hand in his, holding it in a firm, yet comforting grip. "And I was kidding. I respect the meaning of your band. You seemed lost in your head, and I wanted to bring you back to the present."

How right he was.

"I'm Cara."

Why had I given him that name? I stopped calling myself that after Stavros died. It was his pet name for me and reminded me of him.

"You look very familiar. Have we met before?" He released my hand and smiled down at me.

He really was very good looking. Especially his slate-gray eyes—they were kind and genuine. He had the controlled aura I expected from a Dom, but it wasn't overbearing or pushy.

"Not that I know of. Besides, you have no idea what I look like under this mask that covers most of my face."

"It's made of lace and gives a peek of the woman underneath. I see beauty and intelligence."

A prickle of awareness went down my spine. That was unexpected. The only time I'd ever had this type of hyperaware physical reaction to a man was whenever Pierce was around. Not even Stavros could call to this side of me. Ours was a gentle, mutually gratifying sexual relationship, never all-consuming or intense.

A door opened near us, and the couple from the scene exited. They received claps and cheers, but their attention was entirely on each other. The Dom lifted the submissive's fingers to his lips and then led her out of the area.

"They're a very intense couple. Wouldn't you agree?"

"Yes. The love between them brought out the raw emotions of the scene." My body still hummed from watching the submissive orgasm.

"You are very insightful, Cara. I'd like to get to know you better. Care to join me for a cocktail?"

I hadn't thought to do anything but observe. It wouldn't hurt to get to know someone who had an idea of the person I was in real life.

Before I could answer, a possessive arm came around my waist and immediately, I knew the reason my body was so charged.

"She's already spoken for."

CHAPTER ELEVEN

Pierce

Amelia stiffened as my palm slid over her abdomen. Her hand gripped mine, but she didn't push it away as I'd expected.

I knew I'd epically blown the conversation with her, but I didn't regret my offer. I hadn't gone in with the intention of bartering for sex or another child, and marriage had been the last thing on my mind. But there I was, watching the play of anxiety on her face, and my mind spoke before I realized what I was doing.

I wanted her, not just physically. I wanted the relationship we'd had where we could talk for hours and never run out of things to say. I missed the security I felt knowing without a doubt no matter what was thrown at us, the other would be there. I knew those were childhood memories, and wishing for the past was not only stupid but impossible. Hell, I was essentially blackmailing her into this. What other choice would I have? I was desperate to have her in my life, to have our child in my life. She was the only woman I had ever wanted to marry, to have a future with.

I was such a fucking pussy.

"Pierce," Amelia whispered. Her fingers flexed on top of mine. "What are you doing here?"

"I own the place. The more important question is what are you doing here?"

I'd watched her on the club monitors for the last hour. Her disguise made her look like any other submissive in the place who didn't want to be recognized, but she could never have hidden from me. I knew every curve of that body.

If Penny hadn't called me, I wouldn't have come here tonight. Her telling me about Amelia was Penny's way of apologizing. We'd have to have a real conversation soon, but this was a start. Penny was one of the few people I couldn't stay mad at. She loved hard and protected harder.

"Pierce. It is good to see you." Ronaldo smiled his know-it-all smile. "I didn't know you'd be in tonight."

The bastard had known Amelia was mine from the moment she'd stepped into the club. He was the manager in charge tonight and would have known something was up when Penny arranged for the guest membership.

When he'd walked up to Amelia and began to flirt, it had taken all my strength not to punch him in the face. The only thing that saved him was the fact he hadn't gotten over his ex and wasn't even closely ready to move on. Their breakup was almost as devastating as what had happened with Amelia and me.

"You know how I like to pop in every now and then."

He gave me a smirk and said, "I take it that you know Cara."

It was my turn to flex my fingers. I hated that name. It reminded me of how Stavros had taken the woman I'd loved and changed her, going as far as giving her a new name.

"You could say that. Wouldn't you agree, Ame?"

"Yes. We know each other." Her voice was too calm, in the way it would get whenever she was in the mood to fight or fuck.

I'd watched her get aroused by the environment of the club and then even more so as she watched Oliver and Farrah. She wanted to be part of this world but was too afraid to take the step from observer to full-on submissive.

She'd rejected my insane proposal, but I knew if circumstances were different, she would have agreed.

She could change her mind—after all, she still needs your silence.

God, I was an asshole.

"Ame, are you ready to go?" I asked in the same ear Ronaldo had whispered into.

I felt her shiver and then nod. My cock immediately took notice.

It couldn't be this easy. She'd been livid when she left the restaurant. I all but expected her to stab me with a knife, if not punch me in the throat.

I couldn't jump to conclusions. She was agreeing to go with me, not to fuck me or give me another child.

"Does that mean you aren't joining me for a cocktail, Cara?"

Bastard loved to give me a hard time, and I usually found his attempts at cock-blocking amusing, but tonight it pissed me off.

He was one of the few people who'd known me during my swim days. He'd stuck by me when I'd self-destructed after Amelia left me, destroying my career and any hopes of returning to the Olympics.

"Thank you for the offer, but I have to decline."

I gritted my teeth as Ronaldo took her hand in his and kissed the top. "Don't let him bully you, Cara."

"I won't." She gave him a dazzling smile.

Ronaldo smirked in my direction. "Enjoy your evening, Pierce."

"That's the plan."

At my words, Amelia lifted a brow.

It was definitely not going to be easy to change her mind.

"Follow me." I shifted Amelia in the direction of a set of pathways leading to private playrooms.

"Where are we going?"

I waited to respond until we took a hallway that happened to be reserved for our VIP members.

"We need to discuss a few things, and I don't want an audience."

"Yes, we do."

We stopped in front of a false wall at the end of the hall.

All of my clubs had private offices disguised in plain sight. Each of the partners had one, including my brothers and Ronaldo.

Hagen and Zack used theirs to conduct business, but Ronaldo and I would use ours as private playrooms, equipped with everything we preferred when indulging in a scene. Over the years, I'd lost myself in too many women to count, hoping to forget the one person who destroyed my heart. It had been a hollow substitution. That was when I changed to women who understood the rules. We'd share a companionship that included kink, and when our time was over, we'd part ways with no hard feelings.

It had been six months since I'd touched someone other than Amelia. Ever since I knew Amelia would be back in my life, the thought of playing with anyone but her had no appeal.

No matter how much I wanted her writhing under me, screaming my name, and begging me never to let her go, I had to tread carefully.

I scanned my thumbprint on the security panel and pushed the wall, revealing it as a hidden door.

She stepped inside and then came to an abrupt halt. "Holy shit."

***

A melia

My heartbeat drummed into my ears as I took in the room. I expected to have a discussion in an office, but not this. The walls were a pale gray with pops of black and white, very masculine, very Pierce. One side had dark cherry wood cabinets, while another had a display of whips, floggers, and paddles.

My core clenched, knowing what he could do with a paddle, especially if I misbehaved. It was punishment wrapped in a delicious mix of pleasure and pain.

There was a sofa in one corner and a large four-poster bed in another.

How many women had he fucked here?

I pushed the thought aside and then felt my breath grow ragged, coming out in short pants as I took in the St. Andrew's Cross positioned in the center of the room. Images of the couple from earlier flashed in my mind, as did the fantasy I'd weaved of Pierce and me.

I jumped as Pierce set a hand on my lower back, making goosebumps prickle down my spine. "Are you frightened, Ame?"

"No." I licked my lips. "This room doesn't frighten me. I haven't agreed to anything other than talk."

He moved around me and toward a desk in one corner of the room. He gestured to a chair and leaned against the desk.

I remained standing, resting my hand on the high back of the upholstered seat.

"Why did you come to my club, Ame?"

"I was curious."

"Was that the only reason?" His blue eyes studied me, searching for any half-truths or lies.

He'd always done that. I couldn't hide my reactions to him or hold anything from his penetrating gaze.

"Yes." I wasn't lying.

However, now that I thought about it, I knew I wanted more insight into the man who was all but blackmailing me into sleeping with him again.

The outrage still lingered, but what solution did I have

other than agreeing to the bargain? Logic said there had to be other ways to gain his cooperation, but at this moment, I couldn't think of a single one that wouldn't expose Christopher's paternity.

Protecting Stavros's legacy came first. The man had given me a future I never imagined. I owed it to him.

"I see." He didn't seem convinced by my answer.

We stared at each other for what felt like hours. The tension between us was thick, almost as if we'd started a scene. My skin tingled and yearned for his touch.

Fuck, was I really going to do this?

"Now to the reason why I wanted to talk to you. The offer." He sighed. "I'm rescinding—"

"I accept," I said, cutting him off.

Surprise flashed across his face and then was immediately replaced with a look that had a slow pulse of need and anxiety starting to build inside me. I'd always had this reaction when he switched from Pierce to the Dominant. Back when I was seventeen, I had no idea why he affected me like this, but now I knew it was the nature of our relationship.

"I need you to be sure, Amelia." His voice was thick with lust.

"This is what I want. But you need to know something before we go further."

I wouldn't go into this tricking him. There were too many lies between us.

"Go on," he prompted.

"There is a very high chance we won't ever get pregnant. I had complications during my delivery of Christopher. There was scarring."

"I know."

"You had me investigated." It wasn't a question. I should have guessed he would have had every bit of information dug up on me the moment he learned about Christopher. Plus, he had Penny's brother Adrian on his payroll, and Adrian was a super sleuth when it came to learning information, especially the things people went to great lengths to hide.

"Yes. I'm willing to take my chances. As you said, Stavros was sterile. We obviously know I'm not. Not once did I go without a condom when fucking you, and we had a child."

I swallowed. "And if I don't get pregnant?"

"Then I'll keep the terms I laid out. You're free to go back to Greece as long as I have some sort of relationship with Christopher. I won't take him from you, but I will be part of his life as a friend, uncle, whatever."

"And you still want to marry me if I'm pregnant?"

"I've never given thought to marrying a woman other than you."

What did he mean by that?

"I don't understand."

"What is there to understand? The one and only other

time I thought about marrying anyone was when I was nineteen." He moved toward me, stopping when he was a foot from me with the chair the only thing between us.

"Oh." I had no idea what to say to that.

"This is your last chance to change your mind." He lifted his hand, cupping my throat and giving it a slight squeeze before he ran his thumb over my lower lip. "You can walk out that door now, and we won't go any further. We can figure out another solution."

I stared into his cobalt gaze and for the first time since I came back, I saw the vulnerable boy I'd fallen so hard for. He'd always acted the part of the hard, overconfident man, but deep down he had his own demons and insecurities.

"I already said I accepted your offer."

"From this moment on, this body." He shifted until there was nothing separating us.

He gripped my waist, and then trailed the fingers on my throat down between my breasts and to my lingerie-covered crotch. "This pussy." He grazed my clit, eliciting a moan. "Every sound of your desire will belong to me."

His palm splayed over my abdomen. "As will the child I plan to put inside of you."

I opened my lips to respond but nothing came out. Pierce stepped away from me, moving to the far end of the room near the cabinets.

"Strip."

I stood frozen.

This was it. I was now back in the world of those desires I'd tried so hard to repress.

He glanced over his shoulder. "I said, strip."

His voice had changed to the thick timbre that caused my skin to tingle and breasts to swell. He took a seat in an armchair and watched me, not saying a word but ordering me to follow his directions or suffer the consequences.

I moved to a chaise, using the back to help me keep balance as I slipped off my heels. Slowly, I opened the threaded binding of my lace corset. Once it was off, I set it on the sofa. Next came my stockings and underwear. In a matter of minutes, I'd gone from Amelia Thanos, international sports promoter-manager, to Pierce Lykaios's submissive.

"Now come here."

Taking cautious steps, I walked toward him. His hooded gaze had my pulse jumping. When I was a foot from him, he settled his hands on my waist, pulling me closer. I caught myself from tumbling by clutching his shoulders.

He traced one of the tattoos on my hip.

The trident.

It was the exact replica of the one he had on his hip. I'd convinced Pierce to get the symbol as a way to commemorate his six gold medals and the name the press had given him as the American Poseidon.

He lifted his head, beautiful blue eyes locking with

mine. There was pain and confusion warring in their depths.

"So I left a mark on you too." It wasn't a question but a statement.

He hadn't a clue as to the marks he'd left on me. When we were younger, I reveled in the torrent of emotions I'd felt for him. Now it was like drowning with no way to escape.

"When did you get it?" His thumb drew circles around the symbol.

I bit my lip, not wanting to tell him.

"Right after Christopher was born."

He stopped his movement, and his hold on my waist tightened. "Why?"

"I was still in love with you. I wanted something to remind me of a happier time."

"Your husband had no problem with you marking yourself with something to remind you of another man?"

"He didn't know I'd gotten it, and by the time I shared his bed, it was part of my body. He never questioned it."

"What about this one?" He studied the Indian-inspired design going the length of my hip and thigh. "Are those boxing gloves, moons, and dolphins intertwined in the pattern?"

I couldn't help but laugh at his confused tone. "Yes. Anaya designed it for me. She said it represents who I am. I had one of Henna's killer drink mixes, and we were in Tahiti.

It wasn't until the next day when I inspected the tattoo that I realized she'd carefully hidden pictures in the patterns. Let's say I was a bit annoyed that Henna took advantage of my drinking featherweight status and let her know it."

"The gloves I understand, but what about the dolphins and moons?"

I looked away, causing Pierce to cup my jaw and turn it back to him.

"It's me, isn't it? The moon calms the sea, and the dolphins represent Amphitrite, Poseidon's wife."

"Does it matter?" I responded.

"I suppose not." He stood, his height towering over me without the aid of my heels. "Take off my shirt."

The mood instantly shifted, and my arousal began to pulse once more.

He watched me as I slowly untucked his fitted black polo from the waist of his dark denim jeans. I lifted the hem, tugging it up. Pierce grabbed the back of the shirt and pulled it over his head.

Holy fuck. This man was perfection. Sculpted muscles everywhere. He hadn't lost the swimmer's build he'd had as a teen, but now he was broader, more solid, more honed. I wasn't the only one with new tats. He was covered in them. Greek symbols strategically mixed with tribal designs from the indigenous cultures of the South Pacific.

I wanted to reach out and trace each one, but I

remembered I wasn't allowed to touch him unless he gave me permission. In a scene, he had absolute control.

"You can touch me." He picked up my arm and set my palm against his chest.

The feel of him under my fingertips had arousal shooting through my entire body. Like the sweetest of aphrodisiacs designed to entice and lure.

My nipples tightened to stiff, hard peaks, and my core flooded with need.

I tried to steady my breath as I slid my hands over his arms, chest, and down his stomach. This was definitely the body of a man who kept in shape. His muscles bunched and flexed with each pass of my fingers.

As I trailed over his chiseled abs, Pierce stopped my movement.

"My turn." His words were gruff, laced with desire.

He cupped my breasts, circling the tips with his thumbs before pinching the hard nipples in an almost too-painful grip.

"Yes," I cried out, tilting my head back and closing my eyes. God, how I loved this. The bite that sent me to a place I hadn't visited in over a decade.

He released his hold, sending a rush of feeling back into my sensitive breasts and making my body sway.

Steadying me, he said, "We're going to have to establish some rules."

He took one step back as if to put a little distance between us.

"Rules," I murmured. "We have rules?"

"Yes. When we last played, we were two idiots with too many hormones to understand the edge of danger we played on. You liked pain, and I loved administering it. You would let me push you to places you probably weren't ready to explore. I know more, and we will never skate the line again."

His tone changed, snapping me out of my haze.

"What rules do you want to establish? I'm not as naive as you believe. I've been going to clubs for years. Just because I've never played with anyone doesn't mean I don't understand."

I'd learned about the rules of safe, sane, and consensual during those first few visits to the clubs in Spain.

"Then what is your safeword?"

I thought for a few moments, and then said, "Olympics."

"Appropriate since it was the Olympics that ended our relationship."

I wanted to argue that point but held it in.

"Hard limits."

"No sharing or public scenes, no knives, blood, or body modification."

"Good thing I'm not into any of that. Anything else?"

"I don't know. You're the only one I've been with like this."

He touched me again, the heat of his hands like a brand against my ribcage. "And the only one you'll be with ever again."

"Pierce," I all but moaned.

We weren't going to get pregnant or have the marriage he seemed to think was a sure thing. But instead of correcting his assumption, I kept my thoughts to myself.

"Now we begin."

CHAPTER TWELVE

Amelia

"You're mine." He pulled me toward him.

He kissed the juncture between my neck and shoulder, then licked the spot before biting down, not too hard but enough to leave a sting.

I arched against him, wanting so much more.

"I own you. Mind, body, and soul."

He rubbed his stubble along my throat.

"I will bind you, paddle you, fuck you, make you beg for more."

My pussy spasmed and I whimpered, "Oh God, yes."

"When we're not together, you'll think about my hands, my mouth, my cock and all the wicked things I do to you and you beg me to do."

His arms came up around my back, drawing me closer to him as he licked up my jaw and then sucked my lower lip into his mouth.

"You will never be able to leave me again."

His mouth covered mine.

God, he tasted like heaven. There was a bit of whiskey mixed with his natural essence. I gripped the back of his head, meeting each of his demands with my own.

The press of his hard, thick, denim-covered cock against my naked stomach had my arousal soaking my cleft and dampening my thighs.

Slowly, he broke the mind-blowing kiss.

I wanted to protest, but the heated look in his blue depths had me keeping quiet.

"No matter what I do, don't move a muscle. Am I clear?"

I nodded.

Here we go.

"Am I clear?" he repeated in a harder tone.

"Yes, Pierce."

"Good."

He crouched down, aligning his face with my bellybutton but keeping his eyes locked with mine. There was a calculating gleam there, reminding me of the boy I'd fallen for when we were barely out of puberty.

"Remember what I said. Don't move. Hands down by your sides, no shifting, no movement."

"Yes, Pierce." I was in so much trouble. Whatever he planned, there was no doubt I'd break his orders.

Deep inside, he wanted to punish me, make me regret leaving him, taking our son from him, and most of all breaking our hearts. His calm, controlled demeanor couldn't hide what I knew was bubbling underneath.

His focus shifted to my C-section scar. He traced the thin, puckered line with his index finger. Then, he followed the faint stretch marks that hadn't faded, no matter the high-end miracle cream I used.

He shifted lower to my damp cleft. There was no hiding my arousal. Licking his lips, he pressed his nose against my mound, inhaling my scent.

I almost cried out but remembered his words to stay still.

"God, you smell incredible. Your scent has haunted me for so many years."

His tongue darted out, tickling my engorged clit. I shifted and immediately felt the sharp sting of a palm against my ass.

"Fuck." I hissed and moaned, wanting more of the pleasure-filled pain. The sting heated my body in a way I hadn't felt since I was barely eighteen.

"Stay still." He smiled against my folds a second before sucking my sensitive nub deep into his mouth. He flicked and circled, sending waves of delicious delight into my quickening core.

My limbs trembled as the onslaught grew more demanding. Pierce dug his fingers into my ass as he devoured my pussy. He plunged his tongue deep into my soaked channel, and I lost all ability to maintain my hold on anything but the euphoria shooting through me. My fingers clutched his hair and my back bowed.

"Pierce. Oh God, Pierce," I cried and moaned as my orgasm overtook every thought in my mind.

By the time I came down, I was limp and covered in sweat. My breath was ragged as my heart drummed a rapid beat into my ears.

"Tsk, tsk." He hummed. "You didn't follow the directions I gave. You have to know there are consequences."

His words snapped me out of my haze, and I quickly realized I was straddling Pierce's lap with my head against his chest and his hard, thick length a brand under my bottom. My arousal cooled between my legs and soaked the front of his pants.

How the fuck had I gotten here? And if one orgasm had me losing all sense of place and time, what the hell would happen when the games began?

I lifted my face to look up at him. There was a smirk on his lips, telling me I'd given him exactly what he wanted.

"It looks like we're going to have to start your training from the beginning." He ran a finger from my forehead down my nose and over my lips. "Wouldn't you agree?" He lifted his brow, and for a brief moment, he reminded me of the boy I'd fallen so hard for.

"Are you going to discipline me?"

Heat entered his gaze. "Do you want me to?"

I squirmed, not sure how I should answer, and then finally gasped out, "Umm. I...yes."

A sense of excitement filled me at the idea of what would happen next. I glanced to the wall with whips and floggers. We'd never used anything like those before, but I couldn't deny I was curious about what it would feel like. Would I enjoy the sting, the burn? Would I crave the bite of the leather as I did in the past?

"No." He gripped my jaw then turned me to face him. "You aren't ready for those. We'll start with things you've experienced before."

He lifted me to standing, holding my waist until he was sure I was steady on my feet. He rose, offering me his hand, and led me to the spanking bench.

I studied the soft leather-covered furniture and felt my heartbeat accelerate as my pussy spasmed and my desire sparked once more.

"You know what to do." The tone of his voice was back to the one that had every nerve in my being firing to life.

I slid my knees onto the padded leg rests, feeling my breath come out in short pants.

"Relax."

I jumped as Pierce set his hand on my back, pressing

me forward until I was draped across the soft, fabric-covered torso rest.

"Sure I'm going to relax, knowing you're about to spank my ass, if not paddle it."

Where the hell had that come from? Shit, we hadn't even started, and things from the past were resurfacing.

"Ame," he said with a warning. "No brat. You aren't ready for that kind of game. When the time comes, I'll be happy to indulge that side of you."

I glanced over my shoulder, and the fire in his eyes had me nodding my agreement.

There was no way to deny he was right. I liked the pain and the pleasure of discipline, but it was too soon to go toward anything that would keep me from sitting comfortably for days afterward. In the past, I'd push Pierce to give me what I needed, to cross lines we should have never touched. Now I was older and knew so much better, but sadly the desire to push the boundaries was still there.

"I'm not going to make it easy for you and strap you down. I want you aware and anticipating every touch, every sting—every strike. Now lower your head, grip the handles, and rest all your weight onto the bench. I have to get a few things."

Tentatively, I relaxed. It would have been so much easier if he'd used the straps I'd seen dangling from the bottom of the bench. But I guessed that was the point. He was training me. Showing me it was my choice to submit, not something he was forcing on me. He knew I loved bondage, the exhilaration of letting another control my body. This wasn't about letting go in that way. It was about making me aware of him and what we had together.

He moved around the room with efficient steps. The sound of drawers opening and shutting caused goosebumps to prickle my skin.

When he returned, he leaned over me, threading his fingers into my hair and jerking my head back.

"What is your safeword?"

"Olympics," I gasped.

A smile tugged his lips. "Do you know how beautiful you look? I've dreamed about you like this."

He was the beautiful one. His blue eyes blazed with desire and his tattoo-covered, honed body made me thirsty to taste him.

Without thinking, I licked my lips.

He trailed his fingers over my back until he reached the globes of my ass, cupping them. His other hand skimmed the tattoos on my hip. His touch was intoxicating, gentle but firm and completely controlled. Then I felt a lightweight object settled on my lower back. There was a long handle angled up my spine, and feathers.

Pierce picked up the object and began to stroke my back. It was a gentle glide meant to soothe. However, it made me so aware of everything around me.

With every pass of the feathers, my body tingled, and

my pussy wept. The gentle caress had my limbs and mind lulled to his movements, ready and anticipating his next tingling touch.

The first strike surprised me, jolting me forward. I hadn't anticipated the slap of the paddle, or the burn.

"Fuck," I gasped and then gritted my teeth tight and squeezed my eyes closed.

The sting intoxicated me as my core clenched and flooded with need. The muscles in my stomach tightened as he rubbed the sore spot and I couldn't help but shift to get his hand where I wanted it.

"Stay still." He pressed me onto the bench with a palm to my lower back, holding me in place. "Count. You get one for every year you kept us apart. And remember, no coming unless I give you permission, or we start over."

Ten. Fuck I wasn't going to be able to hold out. One tap against my clit and I'd go over. It had always been like this. The pain and the pleasure too much for me to hold back.

I released a deep breath. I could do this. If I could train for hours and hold my own with Neya in the ring, I could control my orgasm.

The paddle came down on my left cheek, and I hissed out, "Two."

He rubbed my ass again. "No, Ame, that first one didn't count, since you moved."

I almost lifted my head to glare at him, but thought better of it and dropped down again.

The paddle struck down in a silent glide but with an unquestionable bite.

"Two." I blew out an unsteady breath and braced myself for more.

The next few smacks came in rapid secession, that had me losing myself in the feel and the euphoria of the pleasure-pain. By the time we reached nine, I was lost in the haze of needing to orgasm and wanting to escape. I dug my nails into the padding of the grips, unable to do anything but wait for the next blow. He'd covered every inch of my ass, grazing my cleft but never fully touching the one place that would send me over. Tears streamed down my face. I needed more, and he was making me wait.

"Please, Pierce. Please," I whimpered.

He pushed a finger into my swollen pussy, sliding it in and out. "God, you're soaked."

I lifted against him, unable to help myself. He worked me with a second finger and then a third, giving me visions of the night a week ago. He worked my swollen, aching pussy until I was writhing against his hand and nearly delirious with the need to come. It was as if he enjoyed bringing me to the cusp of release and then changing his rhythm so I couldn't go over.

If he didn't let me come soon, I'd weep or punch him. Fuck, I was already crying.

"Do you want to come, baby?" he asked as he pulled his fingers free of my soaked entrance.

"Yesss." All I could think about was coming.

"Come, Ame. Let me hear your release."

The paddle landed directly on my pussy, shooting waves of sensation, pain, pleasure, elation through every nerve in my being. I spasmed and convulsed, thrashing my head back and forth. My nails abraded the soft leather under my fingertips. After what felt like an eternal orgasm, the tight coil of need eased, letting me melt onto the bench.

I kept my eyes closed, focusing on the lingering sting. Why was this something I craved? Why was it something I needed? I wanted more, but logically I knew it would be too much. Why wasn't I feeling guilty for having this with Pierce and not with Stavros?

"That was fucking beautiful." Pierce crouched in front of me, lifting my chin to cover my lips with his.

The kiss was gentle but no less passionate than if he'd devoured my mouth. More tears cascaded down my cheeks, and a hiccup escaped my lips.

"Shhh," Pierce soothed. "Don't think too hard. You always were emotional after discipline."

He lifted my hair off my back and to one shoulder, running his fingers up and down my tender bottom. My arousal cooled between my legs and on my thighs, reminding me there was so much more to come.

He moved behind me, and the sound of rustling

clothes reached my ears. A few seconds later, I felt his naked body behind me, making mine awaken from its post-orgasmic slumber.

"Are you ready for me, Amelia?" He ran the length of his thick, hard cock through my wet cleft and pressed slightly into my swollen core as he grasped my hands and clasped my wrists to the base of my spine. "You can still tell me no."

He was bare, no barriers between us. I'd wanted to feel him skin to skin.

There was no doubt in my mind he'd stop, even if it killed him. All it would take was one word. That was what I should do. Say "Olympics" and end this. End whatever this was that would only cause both of us unending heartache.

But instead of ending this, I said, "Please. I need you."

"You just sealed your fate." He slammed into me.

"Yes. Oh God, yes," I cried out as my mind clouded with need and desire.

"Christ. You feel so good," he said through clenched teeth as he held my arms tight and pulled out and pressed back in.

He fucked me slowly at first, letting me become accustomed to his girth and length. And then his thrusts grew harder and faster. The pleasure was beyond anything I could have remembered, hot, rough, and fierce. My body thrashed against the bench, wanting to push back, meet each thrust for thrust. But all I could do was take it, accept his hard, unyielding demands.

My pussy quickened, first with tiny pulses and then with hard spasms, gripping his cock with each plunge.

Pierce slid a hand between my folds, finding my aching clit. The second he grazed the sensitive nub, I detonated, throwing my head back and crying out my release.

"That's it, baby. Let it all out. From this day forward, your pleasure belongs exclusively to me."

He continued to pummel my swollen sex until another orgasm was upon me and we both shattered together.

CHAPTER THIRTEEN

Pierce

I woke to the feel of wet heat engulfing my rock-hard, throbbing cock. The last thing I could remember was falling asleep in Amelia's apartment with her satiated body tucked against me.

"Ame," I gasped and gripped her hair, trying to wake my brain and catch up to my dick.

She hummed as she bobbed up and down, licking, sucking, and teasing with each pass.

She gazed up at me with a wicked smirk, swirling her tongue over the bulbous head of my shaft.

How could I forget how much she loved to suck me off? It was the one area where she demanded to be in charge. I could tie her, bind her, and chain her but the second her lips wrapped around my cock, I was a goner, letting her control the show.

She held the base, pumping up and down, as her tongue dipped into the slit on the top of my shaft. My back bowed from the delicious sensation, and I lifted my hips to guide her in the rhythm I wanted.

She ignored my silent demands and jerked my dick to her torturous pace while her tongue followed the thick vein running the underside of my length.

"Christ."

The sensations were incredible, something I could definitely get used to waking up to every morning.

She was a goddess, gorgeous without a stitch of makeup, beyond anything I could ever imagine. And her body was meant for a hard fucking, toned muscles and soft skin and an appetite for sex that matched my own.

"Mmm," she hummed as she bobbed up and down.

The smell of sex permeated the room, making my cock grow harder.

She rocked her body back and forth with the movement of her head, telling me she was as aroused as I was and was trying to use her fingers of her left hand to give herself some relief.

I could almost taste the sweet honey pooling between her legs and dripping down her thighs.

"Turn around and bring that pussy here. I want to eat

your cunt while you suck me off." I tried to shift her, but her grip on my dick tightened, making me hiss.

"Shh. I'm busy. I'm in charge now." She took me to the back of her throat.

My eyes nearly rolled to the back of my head as she did that swallowing thing no other woman had been able to master. How the hell she didn't choke was something I had yet to figure out.

I bucked up, unable to control my reaction, and fisted the tresses tangled in my fingers. This was heaven and hell all tied in one.

I heard a mewled moan from her as she pressed her thighs together and continued her delicious torture. Next time, I'd tie her to the bed and wake her with my mouth between her legs.

A tingle shot up my spine, the telltale sign I was about to lose control.

"Slow down, or I'm going to come."

She pulled off in a wet slurp and said, "That's the point," before she took me deep again.

She continued to work me hard with her mouth, her hand, her tongue until all thoughts disappeared, my balls drew up in an almost painful spasm, and my cock grew harder.

I clenched my eyes as my orgasm took over and I lost control. I pummeled her mouth, pumping hard and fast, unable to hold back.

"Fuck. Amelia," I gritted out, coming in thick, hard spurts, and holding her down onto my cock until she took every last drop of my cum.

Once I could function again, I loosened my hold on her hair and Amelia released my cock, dropping to her side and resting her head on my thigh.

"Come here."

She lazily crawled up my body. I cupped her beautiful face, drawing her swollen lips to mine. Tasting myself on her lips gave me a heady sense of ownership, and the way she was staring at me when I pulled back said she felt it too.

I opened my arms, and she immediately settled against my body. She pressed her palm to my chest.

"That was hot. I love it when you lose control." There was smugness in her voice.

"Proud of yourself, are you?" I stroked her back.

"Absolutely."

"Now spread those legs," I ordered, sliding my palm between her desire-soaked thighs.

She gasped as I grazed her swollen pussy lips. "This was about you."

"It's still about me." I pushed a finger into her heat, circling it upward until I heard her breath hitch. "I want your orgasm. I want to feel how your cunt ached as you took my cock deep."

My thumb circled her straining clit as I pumped in and out, adding a second finger.

"Oh God, oh God, oh God," she chanted.

Her back arched, and her fingers dug into my arm. The flush in her cheeks deepened, and she bit her just-fucked lips, making my cock twitch from its semi-comatose state.

"More, Pierce. I need more."

"Say it. What do you need?"

"Bite me, pinch me, something. I need it. You're the only one who can give it to me."

That did it. My cock was hard again. She trusted me with her darkest desires. Her need to float. Her need for the edge of pain mixed with her pleasure.

I repositioned my fingers, thrusting into her sopping pussy as I pinched her distended clit, holding on for a few seconds and releasing the moment I felt the clamping of her glorious cunt.

She screamed my name, bucking and writhing as her nails scored my skin.

I held in my wince and reveled in her gorgeous face and body as she lost herself in her orgasm.

Watching her come apart would never get old.

When the last of her spasms ceased, she went limp, eyes dilated and breath ragged.

I withdrew from her swollen pussy, licking her juices from my fingers, and tucked her to me, trying very hard to ignore the raging hard-on wanting me to flip her over and fuck her raw.

Cupping her head, I kissed her temple. "Rest, baby."

"Good idea." She yawned. "I think I'm going to take a nap. Then we can order room service. They have the best pancakes..." She trailed off.

I studied her and realized she was fast asleep. The woman could fall asleep faster than anyone I knew.

Some things never changed. Then again, she needed her rest. This wasn't the first intense orgasm I'd wrung out of her in the last ten hours. I'd taken her four times last night.

I could have sworn I'd worn her out, but it looked as if she was as sex-starved as I was. And her uninhibited need for the tinge of pain was a heady mix for the sadist in me.

Especially tying her down and watching her eyes glaze over right before she completely let go was something I would never get tired of seeing.

Even after the intensity of the scene at the club, the second we'd arrived at her penthouse, we were like animals in heat. I'd bound her, spanked her, fucked her, owned her. She'd given me absolute control, trusted me in a way I'd thought I'd only imagined in my memories.

Had she been like this with Thanos? My research told me Stavros Thanos had been an international playboy with a plethora of beauties on his arm after his first wife had died. The European press liked to say the young American had tamed him, turning him into a family man. The idea made me clench my teeth.

God, what was wrong with me? I was angry at a dead man.

Focus on the woman in your arms, asshole, and not the past.

Amelia shifted, snuggling against my side, and whispered, "I love the way you smell. I missed you so much."

Her words had my heart clenching. I set my hand over the trident on her hip. She'd marked herself to remember me.

Why couldn't she have trusted me? I would have given up everything to be with her. She was the one person who'd been mine, who calmed the anger I'd felt at Collin and even my own mother for allowing the shit I'd had to go through.

The one thing the tabloids had gotten right was Amelia's effect on me. A few words from her or a simple touch and things settled inside.

When she'd left, I'd all but imploded. Nothing anyone could say or do could have kept me from all the reckless things I'd jumped headlong into, from nonstop parties to sportscar races to base-jumping while drunk. If it hadn't been for my brothers, especially Hagen, I would have probably killed myself with my antics.

Hagen had gone as far as locking me in a rehab facility

with his fellow mafia enforcers as guards to get me sober. When I'd come out, I'd learned to channel all my rage and need for control into business and the kink clubs. The clubs specifically gave me an outlet for the desires and emotions I'd discovered with Amelia, especially the years of training under well-respected Dominants.

I wasn't going to lie to myself and pretend the old feelings weren't resurfacing. I'd never gotten over her, no matter how many women I'd taken as my submissives or fucked.

God. How was I going to handle it if she left me again? *She's not yours to keep, asshole.*

The only way to ensure she stayed was to get her pregnant. Then I'd have her and both of our children. But her getting pregnant again was a long shot. I'd read the medical reports Adrian had managed to uncover. The trauma of a thirty-six-hour delivery and the emergency caesarean section had left her uterus in a fragile state.

The one thing I could say without a doubt was that she had integrity. She could have hidden her possible inability to have another child from me. Instead she set all the chips on the table.

I knew if I had been in her shoes, I'd probably let me think we could have a child together and then leave when it didn't happen. But then again, I was an asshole.

Maybe I had some of Collin in me, after all.

No, that wasn't fair.

Collin had been the victim of so much betrayal. Hell, we both had. We'd both learned in the most painful way that the women we loved betrayed us.

I never in a million years thought I'd have sympathy for the man who'd thrown me out as an eighteen-year-old. The man who'd forced me to find my way in a vicious sporting world. He'd done it all to protect us. And the little girl I'd grown up around but never knew was my sister.

Thinking back on my childhood, I can still remember how Anaya had wrapped all of us around her finger, getting us to have tea parties when she would visit us with Lena Anthony and Henna. She looked so much like us, and I never saw it. I always assumed the reason her skin tone was so fair compared to her sister's was because of her North Indian grandparents, not because she was biracial.

Now everything made so much more sense. The way Mama would stare at Anaya and the cold formality between Lena Anthony and Mama.

Maybe it was better that I hadn't known of Christopher's existence. I couldn't image what it must have been like for Mama to see Anaya and not being able to love her as a mother could. Or what it was like to see her friend be the mother she should have been. Hell, what was it like for Lena, raising a child who wasn't her own from a man who betrayed her with one of her closest friends?

I wanted to hold on to my hate for Collin so much.

He'd done horrible things, but it was all to protect his family from Draco Jackson.

The sad part of the whole situation was that I couldn't fault Draco's role in this. He'd handled losing millions to Victor Anthony's schemes a lot better than he could have. He was a mobster and reacted like any boss of an organized crime syndicate would. He'd wanted compensation for his losses, and instead of putting out a hit on everyone involved, he wanted Anaya as payment.

If Collin hadn't hidden Lena and her girls, my life would have been drastically different, my brothers' lives would have been different. However, because of the choices Collin made, he'd had to sacrifice his own family as payment.

Amelia murmured something in her sleep, bringing me back to the present.

My arms tightened around her. What the hell was wrong with me? I had the woman of my dreams wrapped around me. This was all I'd thought about for years.

A yawn escaped my lips as I settled more comfortably onto my back. My future was in my arms. Whether she believed it or not, everything else would sort itself out in time.

CHAPTER FOURTEEN

Amelia

I arrived at Ida a little past four in the afternoon. The plan was to have drinks with Penny and the girls. This was the first break I'd allowed myself since the night I'd ventured into Pierce's club.

Coordinating a fight while overseeing Thanos International took more of my time than I wanted it to, leaving little time outside of my nights with Pierce for anything personal.

Celebrating Henna's baby sister Anaya's admission to an international law summer study program in Geneva gave me the perfect excuse to put work aside for one evening. Especially since none of the girls would ever let me hear the end of it if I skipped out on them.

It was something the college sophomore had vied for since before she started school at the University of Nevada. It was an extremely prestigious program that took less than point five percent of the forty or so thousand people who applied.

"Welcome, Mrs. Thanos. Ms. Kipos asked me to take you to the botanical gardens. She's in a conference with the horticulturist and will meet you by the orchids."

"Thank you. I know the way. I'll head over there." I stepped out of the car and took the ticket the attendant gave me.

I made my way into the opulent hotel. This definitely was the crown in the Lykaios brothers' hotel empire. It was also an opinion I planned to keep to myself. From what I'd deciphered, the brothers liked to one-up each other on who had the best property. It was a game of sorts, where all of them ended up winning since all of their businesses were joint ventures.

It had been such a short time since this thing between Pierce and me started, and it felt like my life was drastically different.

I knew outwardly I was the same woman, but inside I had this need to be with him, to feel his touch, to let him command me and give me the pain-laced pleasure I only trusted him to wield. He was like a drug, and I couldn't wait to get my next fix. This need for him scared me to death. It had taken me so long to get over him the first time. How was I going to handle it when we ended again?

And it would end. What kind of relationship could we have? He'd essentially blackmailed me into sleeping with him again.

Who was I kidding? I'd walked into my affair with open eyes. Pierce would never hurt Christopher by exposing the truth. Hell, he'd given me an out that first night at the club.

Our relationship wasn't all about sex. We seemed to have fallen back into the pattern of talking for hours, sharing stories, and discussing things on our minds. It was easy and effortless. He'd respected my opinion when I gave him pointers on ways to guide Hugo's training without coming off as overbearing.

It felt like we were in a real relationship. Not one that had an expiration date. But even if I wanted to stay, I had responsibilities to Thanos International that required me to be back in Greece.

I tucked a stray hair behind my ear, adjusting my purse on my shoulder before taking a pathway leading to the internationally renowned botanical gardens.

I shook my head. Hagen had wanted Penny so much that he'd built a resort wrapped around all of the things his Starlight loved.

And Penny loved plants. The woman was obsessed to the point of putting herself in danger to get the right species of Elderflower for her unique whiskey concoctions. The lengths she'd gone to for her experiments had given me heart palpitations over the years. Thankfully, the crazy woman had agreed to let a few of my friends who were agents for various security and spy organizations around the world to become her protection detail whenever they weren't on assignment and she got the urge to traipse across the world for her unique plants.

I wouldn't lie and say I wasn't glad the burden of worrying about her had now passed to Hagen. He would make sure she was protected, whether Penny wanted it or not. One didn't grow up as a mob enforcer without understanding the need for security or making sure all those one loved were protected from danger. I wouldn't say Penny was helpless. She was a badass when it came to her safety. My friends and I had made sure Penny was versed in the latest and greatest self-defense methods, much to Hagen's dismay.

I smirked. My best friend was probably giving the gorgeous, brooding man gray hairs.

I approached the doors to the area housing the gardens and a well-dressed guard with a bright smile opened the door and said, "Welcome."

I returned his greeting and made my way to the orchid sanctuary. I inhaled deeply, taking in the fragrant scents of all the flowers. No matter how much I wanted to deny

Penny's saying that a beautiful garden could relax the soul, it was true. There was a sense of peace here.

I found a bench, set my purse down, and crossed my legs, leaning back. I studied all the various labeled plants and then caught sight of a flower named Starlight Sunburst. It was some kind of hybrid of an orchid and gardenia. It was in its own habitat so it wouldn't cross-pollinate into any of the plants that were sectioned based on various regions of the world.

God, what would it be like to have a man love me so much to have plants imported that had my name?

A pang of guilt hit me. Stavros had done so much for me by giving me a life I could never have imagined. And Pierce... He had loved me so much that it destroyed him when I'd left.

I pinched the bridge of my nose. I couldn't live in the past. I had to focus on what was happening now, which was complicated enough. In addition to being lovers and parents, we were competitors in one of the biggest title fights ever organized. The latter part was actually the easiest of all of our entanglements. Business and personal seemed never to cross. When we were alone, there was no Thanos Sports or Lykaios Promotions.

"May I take a seat?" I heard someone ask from my side.

I looked up to find an older Japanese man. His face was weathered and body slim, but he carried himself as a man with a strong will and stamina.

"Of course." I gestured to the empty space near me.

He sat down, stretching his legs out. He nodded toward two young men in suits, who immediately bowed and moved away, but at a distance they could keep an eye on the elderly man. Then I noticed a few other men walking casually but into position as if they were ready to protect their charge at the slightest hint of worry.

At the same time, I noticed my security move into place in a warning to the other men that I had my own protection.

I turned my attention to the man next to me, studying him. His hands were covered in tattoos, many of them in designs I'd seen in various Asian artifacts. That was when it hit me. Was this Draco Jackson, the mobster? I knew the man kept an eye on Hagen and Penny, but what could he want to talk to me about? Yes, I was friends with Lana Kimura, his granddaughter, but that was a friendship developed through Penny, and very few people knew about it.

"This place is soothing, don't you think?" he asked.

"It is. Hagen created something remarkable. It is easy to get lost in the scents and unique plants. I cannot wait to bring my son here."

Shit, why'd I bring Christopher up?

"You have a son?"

"I do. He's the light of my life."

"As it should be. I have five sons, fifteen grandsons, and

one beautiful granddaughter. Although none of them have seen fit to give me great-grandchildren."

I smiled to myself, thinking about the number of times Lana would complain about her family smothering her. When I'd first met her, I hadn't known who her family was and only knew her as Penny's feisty lab partner at the University of Nevada. It wasn't until Penny told me about an incident when she, Lana, and a few friends went away for a weekend in Miami and got in trouble that I'd learned Lana was the infamous Draco Jackson's beloved granddaughter. Draco had personally decided to escort the girls back to school and had given each of them a lecture on propriety.

It was crazy to think I was friends with a notorious mobster's granddaughter, a granddaughter who was as straight-laced as they came, making sure everything and anything she did was always on the right side of the law. Maybe it was her family's antics that made her run the opposite direction.

"I bet your granddaughter has you wrapped around her finger."

A giant grin covered his face, making him look twenty years younger than his reported seventy-six years. "That she does. If I didn't love her so much, I wouldn't have agreed to let her have her wedding in Bora Bora. She's lucky the Lykaios brothers are agreeable and arranged all the details to make it as worry-free as possible."

I bet he twisted Zack's arm in one way or the other to make Lana's wedding happen.

"I'm sure it will be a beautiful wedding. I love Bora Bora. Any wedding there can't be anything but perfect." And it was probably my fault Lana wanted her wedding in Tahiti.

On one of Penny's trips to visit me, Lana had tagged along. We'd spent a lot of time discussing her engagement, the number of people that had to come because people had their feelings hurt if you didn't invite them, and venues to hold the crazy amount of guests. That was when I just threw out the thought of having a destination wedding. So only those who really wanted to be there came.

We hadn't discussed it again until I received a save-the-date with HPZ Bora Bora as the location of the nuptials.

"It better be. That girl is probably responsible for more than fifty percent of the gray hairs on my head." He rubbed his salt-and-pepper-covered scalp. "She is a bit of a free spirit."

"I guess with so many men around her she wants to assert her independence."

He snorted. "Then she chose the wrong man to marry. Her fiancé is as bad as we are when it comes to her protection. If I wasn't sure the man loved her, I'd never have chosen him for her."

Lana's fiancé, Travis, gave Lana the space to be herself without smothering her, something her family had never quite managed. Travis was a well-known international financier, with a reputation for liking control and order. The only place he softened, as Lana liked to tell us, was with her. She would joke he was mush in her hands.

"Sometimes a person who is the exact opposite of oneself is the perfect fit for the other."

Pierce and I were so different—exact opposites, actually. Where he was volatile, I was controlled. Where I wanted to let go, he was disciplined. These last few days with him had shown me how much. We balanced each other, in a way I hadn't realized we'd done when we were teens.

"True, true. My wife reminds me of our differences often enough." He laughed. "People think I'm scary when riled. They should see her when she loses her temper."

I couldn't imagine anyone yelling at the notorious Yakuza leader.

Draco turned his face toward the glass enclosure housing a white orchid with tips that looked as if they were dipped in blood. There was a crease between his brows, and his shoulders slumped as if a sad thought passed through his mind.

"Is something troubling you?"

He remained quiet for a few seconds before he said, "You could say that. Have you ever made a decision that you regret?"

Immediately I thought of Pierce.

"Yes. We all do."

"Not me. You see, I'm the type of man who makes decisions based on analysis and costs. But recently I've learned my way of handling things has resulted in consequences I didn't anticipate."

Okay, this was getting weird. Was a man known for not having a conscience dealing with guilt and regret?

"Want to tell me what happened? My friend is probably lost in her world of plants for at least another thirty minutes."

Penny was punctual in every aspect of her life except when it came to her plants and research.

He tilted his head, his deep onyx eyes taking me in.

"Many years ago, I came to this country with a dream to be different from what I'd known all my life. I worked hard, followed the rules, and dealt with the world as it appeared. However, my past came back, and instead of fighting to keep the new life that I'd created, I accepted the ways of my family and past. With the help of those in my mother country, I became a very wealthy and powerful man here in Vegas and other parts of the country. Eventually, I married a woman chosen for me and had a family, raising them in the old ways."

He paused as if to gather his thoughts. After a few seconds, he sighed and continued his tale.

"Then one of my associates, a man I trusted with my money and business, defrauded my family and me. His betrayal resulted in losses not only for me but hundreds of others. It forced me to take matters into my own hands and resolve the situation in the ways of my ancestors.

"My anger was so great at the man that I wanted to hurt anyone and everyone who was associated with him, blaming them for even knowing the man. This included his friends and family. In the process of my retribution, I destroyed countless people's lives. I viewed it as the cost of betraying me. I can admit that I'm not a very forgiving man.

"Now, many years later, I am learning my actions have cost me a boy that I think of as my own. A boy who viewed me as the father he never had. A boy who I'd taken as collateral damage against those who stood between me and my vengeance."

Dear God. He was talking about Hagen.

Penny had told me Hagen had cut nearly all ties to Draco, and Draco hadn't taken it well. She never divulged any real details except that what Hagen, Pierce, and Zack believed had happened with them and Collin wasn't the truth. It had been all orchestrated by Draco as payment for Collin's involvement in Draco's personal business. Now Draco's words filled in the pieces of the information Penny had given me.

I also noticed he wasn't apologetic for taking Hagen, but the consequences of the truth coming out.

"Is there no hope of reconciliation?"

"We can only hope. The boy is stubborn, much like his biological father and me."

Immediately, my mind filled with so many questions I wanted answered to help me understand Pierce and all he'd been through as a child. But could I ask a man who looked like a sweet old grandpa but was cold-hearted and wielded power like a blade? I wasn't stupid enough to think of Draco as harmless, no matter how frail and calm he seemed.

Part of me wanted to demand Draco tell me if he'd forced Collin's hand when it came to Pierce and me, but the rational part of me knew I couldn't go there. Besides, deep inside I was positive Draco was the catalyst for all the pain and suffering I'd gone through as an eighteen-year-old.

Thinking of the past caused a surge of anger to bubble up, but it calmed just as fast as I remembered the beautiful life I'd had with Stavros. Something that wouldn't have been possible without the events of the past.

"Do you believe an old man who's lived his life without apology can redeem himself in the eyes of those he's hurt?" Draco broke the silence. "Could you forgive a man for changing the course of your life as payment for a crime you didn't commit?"

I studied him and swallowed. Was he asking me to forgive him for his part in what had happened with Collin, or was it a general question?

Fuck, this was not what I'd been expecting when I'd come here. I was going to need at least five drinks to calm my nerves after this conversation.

That was when I remembered what Stavros had said when I'd finally stopped mourning all that I'd lost with Pierce. *"Sweet Amelia, holding on to the hurt and anger of the past only damages you. Let it go, baby. Free yourself."*

Regret burned the backs of my eyes.

I never deserved a man like him, but I was so thankful God had seen fit to bring him into my life.

"I believe if you are sincere, time will heal all wounds. It doesn't mean there won't be consequences or that you won't have to wait awhile, but stay patient. I'm sure things will work out. My late husband taught me that."

Draco took my hand in his and squeezed. "The man you married. He was a lucky man."

I shook my head. "No. I'm the lucky one. He's the reason I'm back here in Vegas. He helped me see that we aren't defined by our past but by how we handle the present and future."

"Then we're all lucky. You do good for an old man's soul. Maybe one day I'll get to meet your son."

I smiled. "Maybe." I lifted my gaze and caught sight of Penny in the distance, worry and concern filling her expression as she took in the man sitting next to me.

"My friend is here." I stood and leaned down to kiss Draco on the forehead. "Thank you, Mr. Jackson, for keeping me company. Lana is lucky to have you, even if you are a tad overprotective. I'll see you at the wedding."

Surprise flashed across his face and then was replaced with a big grin. "You knew who I was the whole time."

"I did."

"Do me a favor. Keep this between us. I'm technically not supposed to be here. The brothers wouldn't like it."

"Your secret's safe with me."

CHAPTER FIFTEEN

Amelia

"Want to tell me what all that was about?" Penny said to me as we made our way to the outdoor lounge near one of the nine pools at the Ida.

I was surprised she didn't ream me with questions the second I reached her after leaving Draco. She'd waited a whole five minutes. I understood her concern, but my conversation was more enlightening than I expected. It also added another layer to the twisted tale of my relationship with Pierce.

Was he aware of what had happened? It also made me wonder how the brothers continued to do business with Draco. But then again, I assumed one didn't just stop doing business with the mob because they were mad at the boss.

"I was just killing time in the garden, chatting with a lonely old man. You're the one who was late because you were too lost in making love to your plants."

"Lonely old man, my foot. Do you realize who you were talking to?"

"I figured it out pretty quickly. You know, with all the scary-ass motherfuckers in suits trying to act like wallflowers but failing miserably."

"And?"

"And what? The conversation helped me understand quite a few things."

"I swear to God, Amelia. If I get in trouble with Hagen over this, I am going to kick your ass."

I smirked. "I'd like to see you try, Mighty Mouse."

It was a running joke between our circle of friends. Penny was the feistiest of us and the most petite. My five-foot-eight height towered over her.

"Where was your security?"

"Around, like usual. They're always with me."

"And they didn't have a problem with it?"

"If they did, they know better than to step in unless I'm in actual physical danger. You do realize I'm always around athletes whose hands are registered weapons."

"I'm serious. Draco is scarier than anything you'll ever face."

"How is it okay for you to be his bud and get him whiskey, but not me?"

"Things are different now. I've made my alliance, and it will always be with Hagen. God, I think I feel a headache coming on. I need a shot or something." She pinched the bridge of her nose. "Hell, I've barely made amends with Pierce for keeping the knowledge of his fatherhood from him. If he found out you were talking to Draco, he would lose it."

"Want to explain why? It's not like I'm privy to any of the Lykaios brothers' business dealings."

Penny shot me a glare. "Are you or aren't you fucking Pierce?"

I winced and glanced around me. "Want to say that a little louder? I'm not sure everyone in the casino heard you."

"You deserve it. You're back together with a man who has ties to Draco's business dealings. Your safety is a higher priority than it has ever been."

"We're not back together. Well, not officially," I responded while ignoring the other parts of her statement. "It's complicated."

She shot me an annoyed look as we approached the attendant at the entrance of the bar.

We followed the leggy blonde to our table.

"All I'm saying is, Draco doesn't just linger in the garden. He sought you out. He wanted something from you."

"Yeah, advice on if those he's hurt could ever forgive

him," I muttered, but Penny caught it and paused, turning toward me.

"Say that again."

"You heard me."

"What did you say?"

"Only that he shouldn't lose hope. That time can heal anything."

"Is that something you believe too or just advice you're dishing out?"

"What's that supposed to mean? I wouldn't be in Vegas if I hadn't forgiven Collin."

"I'm not talking about Collin, and you know it. Are you back with Pierce hoping he'll forgive you?"

I almost denied that I was back with Pierce again. "Forgiveness isn't something we discuss. We tend to avoid talking about the past. There is a lot of pain there for us. Besides, we both know the terms of our agreement. It's the only way to make sure neither of us gets hurt."

"If you actually believe that, then I have a bridge to sell you. You two are playing Russian roulette with your hearts. You're in love with each other and pretending you're not. Hurt is written all over it."

We stopped our conversation as Henna and Anaya jumped up from their spots at a high top overlooking the Vegas Strip.

"It's about time you bitches got here." Anaya engulfed both Penny and me in a tight hug.

"Woman, in Europe I know it's legal to drink when you're under twenty-one but not here. Hagen could get in serious shit if you're caught." Penny glared at Anaya and then at Henna. "You condone this?"

"Pipe down." Henna handed Anaya a twenty-dollar bill. "Anaya said she could get you riled up and she did. You're so straight-laced and uptight sometimes."

"She's got you there." I started laughing. "You must have some crazy bedroom skills to have the man known as the Master of Sin wrapped around your finger."

"You're one to talk," Penny countered. "What kind of games are you playing with the man known as the Master of Games?"

"That's right. I heard rumors that you two had hooked up. Please tell me it's true." Anaya folded her arms as if she were praying. "Does that mean you're into..." She trailed off, wincing, and then shivered. "Never mind, I don't want an answer to that part."

I rolled my eyes and took the vacant seat next to Henna.

"I do." Henna sat up in her seat and leaned in my direction. "Are you into the light side of kink, or is it naughtier?"

A waiter placed a set of drinks in front of Penny and me. I glanced in her direction, lifting a brow, and she shrugged and smiled.

She definitely had the six-foot-five eldest Lykaios brother wrapped around her finger.

"I'll share my personal life, if you share yours," I said to Henna.

She liked to act like her life was mundane, but I knew better.

"What personal life?" She picked up her cocktail and sipped. "I work, sleep, and hang out with you gals when I have a free moment. You do realize I have more on my plate since your ass decided to organize a fight in Vegas?"

"Bullshit," Penny and Anaya said in unison.

"Tell me, when was the last time I did anything for fun that didn't involve hanging out with one of you?"

"Last night at the poker game with those sharks you like to court," Penny answered.

"That was work." Henna frowned. "I have to woo the whales so the Lykaios brothers don't get the upper hand."

"Not buying it," I said, knowing what my girl had been up to. "Who was up until four this morning playing against one particular Lykaios brother?"

"He put a bet on the table. I couldn't refuse." Henna's eyes widened as she realized what she'd said. "How did you... who told you? Oh fuck. Pierce told you. It has to be more serious than bedroom gymnastics if you guys actually talk."

One day soon, the fiery chemistry between Zack and her was going to explode. They may be on opposite sides of the world of casino empires, but it wouldn't stop them from burning up the sheets.

Anaya smacked the table, bringing my attention back to her. "So you are boning the hot-tempered Master of Games?"

Henna smirked, knowing the spotlight was back on me.

I ignored Anaya's question and said, "For the record, he really hates that title."

"The least you could do is indulge my curiosity. I'll be gone for the next four months. I need some juicy gossip to tide me over until I'm back home."

I lifted a brow. "That is what all those magazines you like to squirrel away are for."

"Fine." Anaya folded her arms and pretended to pout. "Since I can't drink, let's order some super unhealthy food and promise to eat it with me instead of complaining about using up a week's worth of calories in one sitting."

God, I loved her. She was the baby sister I never had and let me play the role of caregiver.

"Oh, to have the metabolism of a twenty-year-old," Penny mused and then handed me a menu.

CHAPTER SIXTEEN

PIERCE

"Cash me out." Hagen frowned, throwing his cards on the table. "I swear I'm going to paddle her ass."

"Penny giving you a hard time?" I asked, setting my cards on the poker table.

Instead of having my weekly rundown with Zack and Hagen, we'd decided to have a poker night with a few of our friends—Ronak, Jackson, and Arran. They happened to all be in town for various things and it gave us the opportunity to hang out.

Ronak was an up-and-coming Hollywood director with a taste for movie starlets. Jackson was the money man behind a lot of the HPZ properties. He was essentially our banker.

And then there was Arran. He was one of my closest friends and the lead singer of Onyx Stone. He was also the most famous and infamous of all of our circle, known for his hard lyrics, good looks, and high-profile romances.

We'd met in college when he was a physics major and had remained friends after we'd both dropped out of school to pursue different careers.

So far, I'd lost close to ten thousand, whereas Zack was up by twenty-five. I swore he had the Midas touch. The only two people I knew who could give Baby Brother a run for his money were Penny and Henna. No, that wasn't true—the only person to hand Zack his balls when it came to cards was Henna.

"You could say that." Hagen clenched his teeth. "Our women are at Nyx."

Our women. I liked the sound of Amelia being mine.

"And that's bad how?" Arran asked.

"They ditched their security and decided they wanted to forgo the VIP section to dance on the main floor." Hagen pushed back from the table and ran a hand through his short hair.

"You're too damn overprotective of your Starlight." Zack shook his head. "Let them have fun. We have people all over the club. They'll keep an eye on them."

"The girls decided to climb in the cages and give the floor a show." Hagen pointed the screen of his phone in our direction.

"Man, they look hot," Jackson commented, garnering a death glare from Hagen.

It was a video of Penny and Amelia with their backs to each other, holding the bars of the birdcage as they shimmied and rubbed their short-skirted asses together. A crowd of men surrounded them, and by all appearances, the women were oblivious to the attention they were getting.

I clenched my teeth. I was going to do more than paddle Ame's ass when I got her alone. She was showing off what belonged to me.

When the video panned to the next cage, Zack jumped up, and fury covered his face.

It was Henna dancing, bump-and-grind style, with one of the male dancers of the club. His hand was on her ass, and they were having a great time.

Anaya was the only one who looked sober, but she was sitting on the bar, kicking her feet and shimmying to the music. At least my baby sister had enough sense not to drink when everyone else was.

God, I had a sister old enough for dance clubs. Wait a second, she was only twenty. She shouldn't even be allowed into the club.

If Hagen didn't say something to Penny, I sure as hell was going to.

"Let's go," Zack ordered.

"Tell us again how nothing is going on between you

two," Ronak said as he stood. "If you two aren't fucking, I'm a monkey's uncle."

"And I'm a prima ballerina," Jackson added, fist-bumping with Ronak.

"Assholes," Zack muttered.

Arran drank down his scotch and rose. "Anyone have a baseball cap? The last thing I need is attention for helping the Lykaios brothers handle their women."

Arran's bodyguard passed him a cap.

"Where's Adrian?" Hagen asked as he began texting furiously.

"Leave him be. He's working on the security details for the fight. That's what we're paying him to do."

"His ass should be watching his sister and keeping everyone out of trouble." Zack grabbed his phone from the edge of the poker table and moved to the doors of the lounge we were in.

"He isn't her keeper." I had to defend the boy. He was only twenty-one and had no control over his sister or her friends.

Zack had a lot to learn if he thought Adrian had any influence on any of those women. The poor boy was their family, but he'd be roadkill if he even dared to give them advice.

We arrived at the club less than fifteen minutes later. The room was packed with a line of at least a hundred waiting to get inside.

A group of well-dressed, model-type women passed Jackson, drawing his attention.

"Maybe you guys should handle this. They're your women. Plus, they don't know us." Jackson smirked and moved toward the dance floor.

Ronak shook his head. "We should go with him and make sure he doesn't get into trouble. It's the least I can do for his help with my last project."

Ronak, Arran, and his security detail followed Jackson into the crowd.

"One day I'm going to enjoy seeing those assholes suffer." I glared at Ronak's back.

"That would mean they'd have to take the idea of relationships seriously." Zack scanned the crowd.

"Last I checked you had a string of women you enjoyed on a regular basis," Hagen said as he zeroed in on the girls.

We pushed through the swarm of writhing bodies and stood a few feet from where Henna, Amelia, and Penny danced.

Anaya spotted us first, jumping off the bar.

I shook my head, and she grimaced as she glanced at the cages.

Hagen and I took positions under Penny and Amelia's cage. They were too busy dancing against each other to notice us.

If we weren't surrounded by people, I'd find the fact

she was locked in a cage super hot. She was a goddess in four-inch heels and a minidress that showed off her killer sculpted legs. Ones designed to wrap around my waist as I fucked her until she was insane.

Sweat glistened on her beautiful face, reminding me of last night as I plowed my cock into her.

Over the last few weeks, I'd fucked her at every opportunity, and she'd met every one of my demands with her own. The second we touched, there was an energy shift. She gave herself up to me, letting me control her pleasure in ways she'd never done before.

Right now she looked carefree and lost in the rhythm of the music. Gone was the ball-busting businesswoman and mother. Gone was the always-in-control former athlete.

As if sensing me, she opened her eyes and our gazes locked. There was no surprise there, just heat, as if she was thinking of me while she danced.

The idea of that had my cock jumping. We weren't planning to meet up tonight, but there was no way I was leaving this place without her.

She moved closer to the bars, rolling her hips and licking her lips.

If we were in private, I'd have her strip for me and then wrap those lips around my cock, something I had no doubt she'd enjoy.

She mouthed, "I want you."

I lifted a brow and smirked. She was drunk and horny.

How had I lived without this woman all these years?

A group of men began to make catcalls and whistle, snapping me out of my thoughts. Before I could respond to the dickheads, I heard what I couldn't mistake as a growl.

Hagen grabbed one of the men by the collar, throwing him back.

Oh fuck. Hagen was cold and calm in any and every circumstance except when it came to Penny. When it came to his pixie-sized fiancée, he was a volcano ready to erupt at any moment.

"Out now," Hagen roared, pushing his way up the platform leading to the cages.

I rushed behind him, as did Zack. From the side, I saw Jackson, Ronak, and Arran coming toward us.

Fuck, this was going to get bad if I didn't get everyone out.

Hagen jerked open the cage door and grabbed Penny by the waist, throwing her over his shoulder.

He smacked her ass and stalked toward the club offices.

"I lost my dance partner." Amelia sauntered toward me with unsteady steps.

I grabbed her around the waist and helped her out onto the platform.

She smiled up at me. "This cage is a lot more fun than an MMA ring. I don't have bruises when I come out."

The woman hadn't done anything but eat and breathe the fight for weeks and even on her night to relax, she was thinking MMA.

I'd never met a woman who worked so hard. When she'd told me that she was the head of all of Thanos International and Chairman of the Board, I'd thought she was kidding. Yeah, she had a CEO running the different divisions, but overseeing a large conglomerate was no easy task. When she wasn't working for her athletes, she was reviewing prospectuses and consulting the heads of the various companies under Thanos at all hours of the day. And then nearly every night was spent with me, which garnered her very little sleep. The woman was a machine.

"You ready to go home?"

"It all depends. Am I in trouble?" She slurred her words.

I'd be surprised if she wasn't passed out in the next half hour.

"Yes. You let others see what belongs to me."

"My dress isn't that short." She frowned, tugging at the hem as she tried to balance herself against me. "The skirt barely comes above my knees. Well, it did on Penny."

How the hell she got into a dress designed for Penny, I'd never comprehend. Outside of her ass, Penny was petite everywhere. Amelia was all curves and hard muscle. A woman designed to fuck and indulge every dirty fantasy I could imagine.

"Baby, with those legs that dress is halfway up your thighs."

I guided her toward the hallway Hagen had taken with Penny.

She blew out an exaggerated breath and then sighed, resting her head on my shoulder. "I guess you're right. I'm a good seven inches taller than her. Hey, I have a secret."

"Want to tell me?"

She nodded and leaned up to whisper in my ear, but her voice was anything but quiet. "I've only been drunk once before and that was on my trip with the girls to Tahiti. In Greece, there are lots of rules, and I was never supposed to drink more than two glasses of anything. Even when I would go to Ibiza with my friends, I never drank. You know tabloids are always trying to get pictures of the Thanoses. It's like living in a Petri dish. Plus, as the head of Thanos International and the Chairman of the Board, I have to keep a respectable image. It's the double standard for being a woman in charge."

"Wasn't your husband known for his parties?"

She waved her hand. "That was pre-Amelia. That's what my grandmother-in-law called it. Plus, Stavros is a boy. Boys can do anything and they don't get the same backlash. It's not fair, just the way it is."

"How are you friends with Penny and not drink?"

"I didn't say I never drank. I said I've only been drunk

once before. I found out today I have a surprisingly higher tolerance than I thought."

"Baby, at this moment, you have none. Let's go."

Amelia dug in her heels, forcing me to stop walking.

"I can't go without Henna and Anaya. That would be rude. We're celebrating." She turned to look at the bar.

Zack had Henna and Anaya cornered. Both women had their arms crossed as he gave them a lecture.

"Celebrating what, exactly?"

"Anaya's new summer internship in Geneva."

"If you're celebrating Anaya, why isn't she drunk?"

Amelia looked at me as if I'd lost my mind. "Because she's underaged. We aren't going to do something to shut down the club."

"Anaya isn't old enough to *be* in the club."

"Well, she promised not to drink, so we snuck her in through the back. Oops." She covered her mouth. "I wasn't supposed to let Hagen find out. Don't let Hagen find out. Okay?"

What was in those drinks they'd downed? Never had I imagined Amelia being a silly drunk.

"I think he already knows."

"Oh no. That means we're in trouble. Are you going to paddle me?" There was a sparkle in her eyes that said she would enjoy it if I decided to redden her ass.

"Not tonight."

She frowned, looking disappointed.

"Then I guess you're taking me home." She rested her head on my chest and closed her eyes. "Mmm. You smell good."

That was my cue to leave. I lifted a hand, signaling Zack and the guys.

Zack nodded and then continued the heated discussion with Henna. Anaya caught my stare and ran toward us.

God, she looked so much like Mama. How the fuck hadn't I noticed it before?

"Pierce, would you please drop me off at my apartment? Those two are going to keep arguing, and I have to meet with my adviser in the morning." Anaya wrung her hands together.

Was she worried I'd say no?

Ever since I found out she was my sister, it killed me not to have a relationship with her.

"Sure. First, help me get this champ into the car. She's asleep on her feet."

About ten minutes later we had Amelia comfortably settled into the back of one of the Ida SUVs with Anaya and me flanking her.

"Just so you know, it wasn't her idea to drink. She's a featherweight. Always has been."

"She already told me." I stroked Amelia's back. "How much did she have?"

"She had two martinis, but then I'm not sure how

many shots of Firewater. I'm guessing somewhere between five and fifteen."

"Fifteen?"

"Well, that's how many Penny and Henna had. They can drink a sailor under the table. Maybe it's because both of them have spent years testing out all of Penny's whiskeys."

"Does it bother you that Henna and Penny are so close?"

She frowned. "Of course not. I'm the kid sister, but they never made me feel like an outsider. Though I do wish I had more family. Penny is the only extended family I have. Everyone else wanted nothing to do with us. It isn't always easy being just Henna, Mom, and me. You know, especially with all that Dad did."

God, what was it like for them to grow up with the stigma of Victor Anthony's crimes?

"Well, you do have us. Hagen, Zack, and I will always be around."

She seemed startled by my words and just stared at me.

"Because of Penny?"

"No, because of you. We like you. Plus, it would be nice to have another genius around who could give Adrian Kipos a run for his money."

"Thank you." She gave me a watery smile, and for a second, I thought I saw longing in her eyes.

Could she know the truth?

Even if she did, this was not the time to ask her.

"Tell me about this internship?"

I carried Amelia into my penthouse and headed straight for my bedroom. She had barely stirred during the drive.

In a sense I was glad I'd gotten the short twenty minutes to drive to Anaya's place to talk to her. She seemed so energetic and carefree, but I got the sense it was a facade. Every so often I'd see a flicker of emotion that told me she wasn't as uber confident as she liked everyone to believe. It was especially evident when I'd asked if she was ready for her crash course in international business. Something about this internship had me questioning what else she was going to do in Geneva besides academia.

I held my tongue, not wanting to open a topic I technically had no business involving myself in, and planned to corner Henna about it at a later time.

That was when it hit me. I had a half-sister, who was a half-sister to Henna, who was first cousins with Penny. And on top of it, my brother was marrying Penny, making all of us related in so many ways that it boggled the mind.

I laughed aloud.

Damn, was this a Greek soap opera in the making, or what?

"What's so funny?" Amelia tilted her head up. Her eyes were still alcohol hazed, but at least they weren't rolling to the back of her head.

"You. I'm never letting you go out with Penny ever again. That girl is a bad influence."

"Not happening. She's my sister in everything but blood. She wants to party, I party." She rubbed her forehead as I set her on the bathroom counter in my master suite. "But I don't plan to ever let her talk me into doing shots every time a man hits on Henna. That woman attracts men like flies to honey."

"Henna is beautiful." I opened a drawer, pulling out a washcloth, and then turned on the sink to warm the water.

"I know." Amelia leaned back until her head rested on the picture-framed mirror above the vanity. "She has the gorgeous skin and expressive eyes of a Bollywood movie starlet, the fashion sense and body of a runway model, and the intelligence of a hunting shark. No wonder she drives Zack crazy."

"Noticed the attraction, did you?" I dampened the cloth in the warm water, added a little soap, and then gently began to wipe the makeup from Amelia's skin.

Why the fuck did she have so much shit on her face? She was beautiful without it.

"It's hard to miss. Neither of them is going to admit it. I think it's because of Collin. Henna adores him, and Zack—well, everyone and their dog knows how Zack feels. He was never good about hiding his emotions, especially when it comes to Collin."

"Zack is Zack." After I finished cleaning her face, I set the washcloth on the counter and pulled out a toothbrush from another drawer.

We remained silent as I brushed her teeth.

Her head rolled to the side toward the wall opposite of us, and then she groaned as she shifted to face me again. "Pierce?"

"Yes."

"I'm still drunk."

"I know, baby. Stay here. I'm going to get you something so you don't have a hangover in the morning."

"Okay. The mirror is very comfy."

I shook my head and quickly went to my kitchen, finding the hair-of-the-dog concoction Zack swore by and bringing it back to Amelia.

She hadn't moved a muscle since I'd left.

"Scoot down and drink this."

She wrinkled her nose as she got a whiff of the drink. "Do I have to? It smells awful."

"Yes, it works."

She swallowed the contents, having to breathe through the foul taste. I handed her a glass of water to clean out her mouth.

"If this is what I have in store for me after a night out, I'm never drinking again."

"Good. Now, I want to take this thing you call a dress off you."

I helped her to standing and unzipped her dress as she dropped her forehead to my chest.

When it fell to the floor, I clenched my teeth. All she'd had under her skimpy outfit was a barely there thong. My cock jumped, wanting nothing more than to turn her around and drive deep inside her pussy.

I released a breath and slid my fingers into her hair, holding her to me.

"Why are you so calm?" she whispered.

If she only knew how far from calm I really was.

"What else would I be?"

"I saw the look in your eyes when I was in the cage. I wasn't sure whether you wanted to discipline me or fuck me."

My cock went from jumping to full salute. The idea of whipping her and then denying her release was a distinct possibility for the future.

"Let's not talk about that now. You need to sleep off the shots."

"Am I in trouble?"

"Yes. You ditched your security."

"No, I didn't. Penny ditched hers—well, the ones Hagen assigned. Mine are always around. Most of the time no one sees them."

"What do you mean they're always around?"

"Stavros has had a team with me since we got married. They're agents from various ops organizations. Whenever they're not on assignment they rotate out to protect me. I'm friends with most of them. A few of them even protect Penny. Do you think I'd let her go into the jungles of Asia looking for her stupid wild elderflowers without security?"

How much shit was this woman dealing with? First I found out she ran an organization worth over one hundred billion while dealing with misogyny and trying to live a super restrictive life where she rarely if ever drank, and now I find out she had a team of black ops specialists as her secret security detail.

"Why haven't you said anything about them?" I walked her toward my bed.

"Because they're supposed to be like ghosts. Most of the time I don't even notice they're there."

"Is there a time when they aren't with you?"

"Only when we're alone. They know you have your own protection."

Thank God for small favors. What Amelia and I did was for us only.

"Pierce, did you know Penny said I talk a lot when I'm drunk?"

That made me smile. She was a quiet person by nature, and hearing her reveal so much without prompting was interesting and refreshing.

"I'm beginning to see this."

I opened the covers and guided her onto the sheets, sliding in fully clothed behind her.

She adjusted her pillow and yawned.

"Rest, love."

"Pierce," she mumbled as she drifted off, "will you hate me if I can't give you a baby?"

I studied her. Why was she thinking about a baby now?

"I could never hate you. Even when I wanted to, I couldn't do it."

"So Christopher is enough, even if you can't claim him?"

It killed me to know I couldn't let anyone outside of my small circle know the truth. And if I was honest with myself, the contingency of another child was just a way to tie her to me.

"Yes."

She cupped my cheek. "Why?"

"Because this is all about you. I never stopped lov..." I trailed off as her eyes drifted closed and she inhaled deep, falling into a drunken sleep.

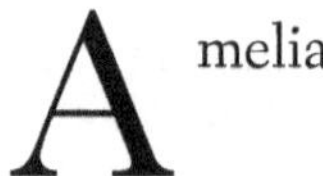

A melia

. . .

My phone vibrated near my head, and all I wanted to do was die.

Who the fuck was calling me?

I searched around for the God-awful device and answered, "Someone better be dead or dying."

"*Amelia, Astros is going to be a problem,*" were the Greek words I heard in response.

"Lucas?" I tried to clear the fog from my brain.

How much had I drunk last night? My body ached, and my stomach wasn't happy either. Hell, the way everything was still fuzzy, I was probably still drunk.

"*Yes, Amelia. I know it is only four your time, but we must talk.*"

"*We have a call set for ten to discuss the board meeting. Call me then. I need sleep.*"

"*Amelia! Wake up. We have to talk now.*"

The urgency in his voice snapped me out of my stupor. I wiped my face with my hand and adjusted the phone with the other.

"*Okay, give me a second for my brain to fire.*"

That was when I felt a hand slip over my stomach, making me freeze.

"Who are you talking to?" Pierce asked and looked at me through sleepy blue eyes.

Fuck. I forgot I'd given Pierce a key. He had to have

come in after I'd gone to bed. Wait a second, I wasn't in my own bed.

I glanced around the dimly lit room and realized I was in Pierce's penthouse. That was when I remembered the night before and my case of verbal diarrhea.

I'd have to deal with that later.

I pulled the phone from my ear, covering the receiver end, and said, "Sorry. I didn't mean to wake you. I'll go in the next room. Go back to sleep."

I slipped from the bed, and then groaned as a wave of dizziness hit me.

Fucking Firewater shots.

After a few seconds to calm my head, I made my way into the hallway, closing the door behind me. I slowly walked toward the giant living room lit by the glow of Vegas below and toward the oversized couch positioned by the fireplace.

After turning on the side-table lamp, I settled under a plush blanket, dropping my head back. I felt like hell and now Lucas wanted to talk.

I loved Stavros's nephew and never regretted leaving him as the CEO of Thanos International. He knew the business better than I ever would, having grown up in it and getting his first job there when he was fourteen as a mail boy. The fact we were the same age and I was his aunt always made me laugh.

Stavros had essentially raised Lucas with Sylvia.

Stavros's brother hated the idea of parenting his child and decided Stavros and Sara should raise his son. Then when Sara passed away, Sylvia had taken on the role.

"Okay. We can talk now. I'm putting you on speaker. I'm too tired to hold the phone."

"Was that a man in your bed or was that deep voice something you're practicing as a possible act if the promoter thing doesn't work?" There was a hint of amusement in Lucas's voice.

"I went out with Penny last night, and I wasn't the proper Thanos wife. Now I'm suffering the consequences and not feeling friendly."

That was when I realized Lucas had mentioned Astros.

"Did you say something about Astros?"

"Yes. The board was split down the middle, as you predicted. When I unsealed your vote and read that you were against the ship port sale, Astros erupted. Saying it was forged and that you had to be present to break a tie."

"That's bullshit. I followed proper procedure detailed in the company bylaws." I pinched the bridge of my nose.

"That is what saved you. You were so meticulous about following procedure that Astros couldn't truly challenge the validity of your vote."

"It's not like I voted to throw him off the board." A position he got because of his friendship with Stavros, not because he brought any value to the company.

"He then decided to tell the board you are tarnishing Stavros's memory by whoring yourself to your former lover."

"That bastard. I'm beginning to hate him, Lucas. I'm not the one with a reputation as a philanderer."

"I know this, Cara. But you and Sylvia are the only women who have ever led the company. They hold you to a different standard than..." He trailed off.

"Than a man. I am so fucking sick of this. So, they expect me to mourn Stavros by staying single and living alone for the rest of my life?"

"Is it serious with Lykaios?"

I hesitated to answer, then said, "Yes."

"They are going to make you choose, and Astros is going to lead the charge."

"So in other words, I have to prove my loyalty to Stavros and his legacy. Prove I'm worthy of being a Thanos."

"This isn't how my uncle would want you to live. There isn't any shame in telling them to fuck off. It's not like they can unseat you. Sylvia is the only one who can do that, and she loves you."

Thinking of my grandmother-in-law made me smile. She'd held her family together after her husband died. I would never want to do anything to shame her.

"Let's see what steps Astros takes before we start expecting the worst."

"Cara, it is the worst. Some of the things he said about

you, I won't repeat. He is using the bias the older members of the board have about women against you."

"I can handle it. The only thing you need to do is handle the tasks I have given you."

Lucas sighed. *"Will do. Is it truly so important to keep Stavros's legacy so pure? He wasn't perfect. He had a reputation of his own."*

"He was good to me."

"Cara. You can't make a decision about your future based on Stavros. If you had to choose between your relationship with Lykaios and the company, what would you choose?"

"No matter how much I would want to make a different choice, I'd pick Stavros's legacy."

"I figured you would say that. Before I let you go, I thought I'd tell you that starting next week you won't be the only woman with access to the all-male halls of headquarters."

I smiled. *"Olivia accepted the job. I'm so happy."*

Olivia was the daughter of Stavros's cousin. She was fun, smart, and ambitious. Plus, she was the first female born into the Thanos family in sixty years, diluting the all-male rule of the clan.

A yawn escaped my lips. *"Lucas, I have to get some sleep. Call me if anything changes."*

"Will do."

CHAPTER SEVENTEEN

Amelia

"Time to wake up, Ame."

"No, five more minutes." I stirred from a deep sleep.

"It's past ten. I can't watch you sleep any longer."

I tried to shift and realized I couldn't move. My eyes flashed open, and there was Pierce, sitting between my splayed legs holding a cat o' nine tails in his hand.

He was naked, his cock hard and thick, curving toward his bellybutton, and there was an almost feral gleam on his face that had my pussy clenching.

I jerked my arms, only to have the bite of metal abrade my wrist. He'd tethered me to the four corners of the bed. I was spread wide open for whatever it was he'd planned.

I felt heat creep up my face, then the knowledge that I was about to receive the consequences of last night's antics.

I felt my cleft grow slick.

The fact I was anticipating the discipline more than dreading it wasn't lost on me.

"Am I in trouble?"

He lifted the cat, running the tails of the whip up and down my legs. The knots on the end sent goosebumps over my flesh. I could almost feel the sting to come.

"Why would you be in trouble?"

"The dress."

"That could be it."

The leather tails glided up my abdomen, circled one breast, and then the other.

My breath reacted to the touch, coming out in short pants.

"Getting in the cage with Penny? My security was there, so nothing would have happened to us."

Hell, they were always around. I couldn't fart without them knowing. Shit, had I told Pierce about them? Maybe he was upset about that.

"That could be a possible reason. You did let others get a view of what belongs to me."

"Then what?"

Instead of answering, he flicked his wrist, and the cat landed on the swell of my left breast.

"Oh God," I cried out as my breath left my chest and I

jerked against the restraints holding my body down. Slowly, the sting seeped into my skin before dulling to a delicious tingle.

Before I was prepared, he smacked the right breast, grazing my nipple. Stars flashed in the backs of my eyes, and a needy groan escaped my lips.

My core began to quicken, and my mind filled with a sense of euphoria.

His lips and tongue laved the inflamed skin, adding to my heightened senses.

"Do you want more?" he asked against my nipple, sucking in the tip until it was straining, hard and achy.

I nodded, unable to voice my need.

He took the handle of the whip and slid it through the arousal seeping from my swollen pussy and moved his attention to my other nipple.

"I can't hear you."

"Please, I need more," I managed to gasp out.

"I'm glad. Because more is exactly what you'll get."

He reached to his side, grabbing something I couldn't see.

"Do you know what these are?"

Two blue and red stone-adorned clips were clasped between his fingers. They were connected by a silver chain and had a charm dangling from the center that said *owned*.

Nipple clamps.

They looked as if they were real jewels. Real sapphires and rubies.

"Yes."

"I had them made for you with our birthstones."

I studied him, not sure what to say. This wasn't something he enjoyed in private. It was a lifestyle. One I would have shared had I not left.

He glided the jewelry between the valley of my breasts —the cool metal a sharp contrast to my heated skin.

With one hand, he pinched one of my nipples in an almost too-painful hold. He released it quickly and attached a clamp, screwing it so I would feel the ache but not lose feeling. He repeated the process on the other breast.

The heady mix of pain and arousal had my mind clouding.

"Beautiful."

His hum of delight sent a tingle up my spine.

"Your body needs one more thing before we begin."

I exhaled sharply. "What have we been doing until now?"

"Foreplay."

I was about to give him a smart retort when he lifted a dark brow.

That was his sign I'd have consequences if I said another word. Something I was positive would involve orgasm denial. It had been his favorite to tell me he was pissed in the past.

"Now, one more thing to get you ready."

He pushed two lubricated fingers into my pussy. "God you're so wet, I probably didn't need to do this."

He pulled out and immediately replaced his fingers with a firm, smooth object.

The dildo clicked on the second it was in place.

"Oh." I moaned, shifting my hips.

The vibration was at a low setting, one designed to arouse, to torture, but not strong enough to send me over.

He lifted up, moving to the side of the bed. His beautiful naked body was on display. He caught me watching him and gave me a heated grin.

"Let's get started."

He picked up the cat, and before I could focus on anything he struck.

SMACK, SMACK, SMACK.

Fuck, that hurt. Tears streamed out of my eyes as fire poured over my abdomen and thighs, filling my body with heated desire.

"More," I begged. "Pierce, I need more."

"Are you sure?"

"Yes. Please don't stop. It's been so long."

"So be it."

Over the next few minutes, the leather grazed, bit, and marked every centimeter of the skin on the front of my body. No part of me was spared, including my bare mound. Whenever he grazed my pussy, he shifted the vibrator, sending me closer to the edge.

My body screamed in wicked pain and pleasure. It felt as if I was on fire, and I wanted, needed more. My nipples ached, my pussy throbbed, my whole being ached for release.

"I need to come. Please let me come."

SMACK, SMACK, SMACK.

I thrashed against the cuffs, and I had no doubt my arousal soaked the sheet under me. My pussy clamped down on the pulsating cock inside me, but no matter how I ground myself against it I couldn't go over.

Just when I thought I'd go delirious, he dropped the whip to the floor and crawled over me on all fours. His weeping cock bounced between us. His hypnotic blue gaze held mine as he lifted a hand to cup my face.

"Who do you belong to, Amelia?"

My breath began to come out in shallow pants. If he didn't hold me or fuck me, I'd lose my mind.

My safeword sat on the tip of my tongue.

He leaned down, biting my lower lip. "Tell me who owns you."

"Right now, you," I gasped out.

I knew it was the wrong answer, but I said it anyway. I would have to go back to Greece, and this was the only way to keep from losing myself entirely in him again. His touch intoxicated me, made me want so much more, and I couldn't give either of us hope for more, especially after the call with Lucas.

Anger and hurt filled his gaze. "Not just now, forever. I am your addiction. I will haunt you. Make you crazy with wanting me. Leaving isn't an option for either of us."

"Pierce, don't..."

I never finished my words as he pulled off the first clamp, and I screamed as feeling rushed to my nipple. At the same time, my pussy clamped down harder on the dildo.

A haze filled my mind and intensified when the second clamp released as I rocked over the crest. I bucked and cried and thrashed, unable to focus on any one sensation or the orgasm I couldn't control.

"Pierce. Oh God. Pierce."

He knelt between my splayed legs and pulled the vibrating cock out of my dripping pussy then replaced it with the crest of his rigid shaft. My body continued to float on the release that wasn't quite satisfying.

"Do you want this, baby?"

"Yes. I need you."

"Do you?"

I clutched my fingers against the cuffs, tossing my head back and forth. "Yes. Please. It's not enough without you."

My mind, heart, and body ached for him. Why was he doing this to me?

He slammed into me, my back bowing but unable to do anything but take his hard, relentless assault. He sank in and out of my swollen, aching tissue. His thighs rubbed along mine with each thrust, but he kept the rest of his body distant from mine.

I ached for more. The orgasm from moments earlier was only half of what I needed. I wanted to feel the connection, the slide of skin, the heat of his body—the taste of his lips. What we'd shared every day since all of this began—except today.

"Please, I need more. I need..."

"I know what you need. But you won't get it. I want you to know what it feels like. I want you to know how much it hurts to ache for something that is right there but you can't ever reach."

He pounded my sex, working me until I was climbing again. Then we both shattered simultaneously, calling each other's names but feeling unfulfilled.

I barely registered when Pierce removed the handcuffs or when he rubbed the feeling back into my limbs. I remained silent as he cleaned my body, rubbed a salve on my skin and then pulled me against him.

This was not how it was supposed to be with us. The kink, the games, the pain was deeper with emotions and need wrapped all around it. What we'd done felt cold, detached.

I turned to my side.

"This wasn't about the club, was it?"

He lifted the arm covering his face and looked at me. "No, it wasn't."

There was a hint of resignation in his voice I couldn't understand.

"Then what was it about?"

"You tell me."

Propping myself on one arm, I said, "I don't know."

"Bullshit." He rolled off the bed and walked toward the bathroom.

I followed behind him, grabbing one of his shirts from the back of a chair and slipping it on. "What the hell does that mean?"

He seized me, pinning me against the wall. "It means you're biding your time until you have to leave. You're expecting it to end. You said as much on the phone this morning. The only fucking times you've been honest with me were when you were drunk or in a scene."

"You listened to my conversation with Lucas?"

"I came out behind you but you didn't notice."

Fuck. I forgot. He was fluent in Greek.

"Did you love Thanos so much that you would let a group of men who seem to despise you run your life? You're not giving us a real chance."

"It's complicated. I have to protect..."

"I don't want to hear it."

He released me and walked farther into the giant bathroom and toward the shower. He turned on the faucet and then stepped back, resting his forehead against the outer stone wall.

"What does it matter? I should have known better. I forced you into this. A child for a child. I'm the bastard who offered you the deal."

I winced inside.

"You're free. I won't force you to give me another child. I won't force you to be something to me that you don't want to be. All I ask is that you let me have some sort of relationship with Christopher. I think it's better if we stay away from each other unless it's absolutely necessary."

A numbness washed over me. This wasn't how it was supposed to end. The last thing I wanted was for this to end.

"Pierce," I said in a soft whisper, "I don't want what we have to stop."

"God, Amelia. I'm trying to do the right thing. I won't let you destroy me again." He gripped the stone edge of the shower wall. His fingers were white from the intensity of the pressure.

Slowing moving behind him, I slid my palm over his stomach, feeling the muscles clench as I pressed my body to his and my lips to his spine, just under the tattoo that covered his upper back.

"I don't want to hurt you. I want to be with you."

"For how long?"

"As long as I can." It was all I could promise.

"What about Christopher? He'll be here soon. What are we going to tell him?"

"At first, nothing about who you really are." Pierce's stance stiffened, so I continued, "Then in the future, when he's old enough to handle it, we'll tell him the truth. He all but hero-worships you. He wants to beat your record. So we'll have dinner together the day after he comes to town. You can get to know him."

"And Stavros's claim to Christopher? To you?"

"For now, it'll remain the way it is. But in the future—I don't know."

My body filled with regret, knowing I wanted Pierce more than I ever wanted Stavros. Logically I knew Stavros had never gotten over his first wife. He'd loved me, but in a different way.

At that moment, Pierce turned, taking me into his arms. He held me as I let the sadness release.

"Am I always going to have to compete against a dead man?"

How could I explain that there was no competition, he had always come first in my heart?

I tilted my head to look at his breathtaking face. "Pierce. Stavros isn't here. I'm with you."

"Are you?"

"Yes." I rose onto my tiptoes, kissing the frown from his lips.

The instant our mouths touched, a fire ignited. We began to devour each other, tasting, savoring, consuming. Our tongues dueled, unable to get enough.

"Pierce," I gasped and then went back for more.

I loved the taste of his kiss, intoxicating and all-consuming.

A groan rumbled from his chest as he cupped my ass, lifting me up against the hard ridge of his growing cock. I instinctively wrapped my legs around him, rolling my hips so the head of his erection slid along the damp length of my cleft.

He carried me into the shower stall, pushing my back to the tiled wall. The steaming spray cascaded down our bodies. Pierce lowered me to my feet without freeing my lips.

He tore the soaked shirt from my body. His need was almost overwhelming, and there was no way I would consider stopping the onslaught.

His mouth trailed down my neck and chest, licking and nipping until he was facing my slick pussy. He licked his lips and then descended. His tongue pushed between my folds. Lifting both of my legs, he set them on his shoulders and continued to consume me. He circled and flicked at my clitoral nub, making it strain and ache.

I had no control, and I had no desire to do anything but let him take charge of my body. I grabbed hold of the showerhead with one hand and threaded the other into his hair.

Water pounded over my skin, adding to the erotic feel of Pierce. The low pulsing deep in my core grew harder, spurring the start of my orgasm.

The second Pierce's fingers pushed into my pussy and curled upward toward the hidden bundle of nerves, I detonated.

"Oh, Pierce." I clenched his thick ebony tresses in a relentless grip as waves of ecstasy poured over me.

Slowly, Pierce rose, still holding me up, and positioned the thick purple crown of his cock at my entrance.

He held my gaze as he thrust forward.

Something in that moment shifted between us. As if the past, the present, and the future were tied to each other.

I slid my arms around his shoulders and drew him closer, kissing him with all the emotion and love I felt for him. He responded in turn. We moved together, loving each other like never before. This time when we came, it was deeper, more passionate, emotional, and soul fulfilling.

CHAPTER EIGHTEEN

Amelia

A couple of weeks after my drunken night out with the girls and my fight with Pierce, I sat on the benches in the Lykaios training facility reviewing a binder filled with open promo spots Thanos Sports was negotiating to fill before the fight in a little over five weeks. I had a handful of high-maintenance sponsors who I knew would sign but needed a bit of hand-holding that took more energy than I truly had to spare.

Plus, Pierce was out of town and I was sexually frustrated.

"So is it serious, or are you scratching an itch?" Apollo said as he approached me.

Apollo wiped his sweat-covered face with the towel

draped across his shoulders and set a local gossip-column page next to me. Front and center was a photo of Pierce and me at dinner two nights ago. His face was too close to mine to be platonic but showing no other outward signs of what was actually happening under the tablecloth.

The headline read: "Definitely More Than Friends."

I could almost feel the slow strokes of Pierce's fingers across the damp crotch of my thong. He'd teased me nonstop throughout dinner, never going further than the slow, sensual torture of his hand. I'd been nearly out of my mind to come. Then the bastard had taken me back to my penthouse and all but pushed me inside, only saying one word—"Training"—before he shut the door in my face and left me there, overheated and desperate to come.

I'd had the urge to handle the situation myself, but knew I wouldn't get the relief I craved no matter how many times I made myself come. Now the asshole was in New York for an important meeting, and I was here working and needing relief.

Fuck training. I hate training.

Taking a calming breath, I traced the photo with my fingertip and said, "It's complicated."

"Don't give me that bullshit. I've known you far too long. I've seen the subtle changes over the last month. Whatever is happening is way deeper than anything I've ever seen with you, and that includes your relationship with Stavros."

I closed my eyes for a brief second, unable to deny the truth of Apollo's words.

What was I supposed to say? That this was more than an itch, it was an unquenchable need to be with, to fuck, to love Pierce Lykaios. I had to get him out of my system before I returned to my sweet conservative life in Greece. A life that I dreaded more and more with each passing day.

How was I supposed to pretend I didn't have the need for the submission, the discipline, the pain-laced pleasure I felt under Pierce's hands? Or the freedom to let him control my world? How was I supposed to go back to a business where every decision I made was questioned because of my sex? Or having to create a company I loved as a way to rebel against the back-assed views of the people around me?

Something had changed on a fundamental level between Pierce and me since that fight at his penthouse. Our private life had made its way into the public.

The world knew we were together. And the games we played were now in plain sight. However, unless we called attention to it, no one would know I was living the lifestyle I had no doubt I'd have lived in if Pierce and I had never broken up.

"Are you going to answer me?" Irritation laced Apollo's words.

"He was my first love. Some of those feelings never die."

"It is way more than rekindled childhood romance. I'm not blind." He crossed his giant biceps and glared down at me. "You two have way too much history. And not the happy kind. I don't want your heart broken."

"If you're about to lecture me on my sex life, sit down. I'm getting a crick in my neck."

He threw his towel on the metal bleacher and stepped across the first row, straddling the bench.

"Ame." He ran a hand through his barely there hair. "How the hell do I say this?"

I frowned. "Just say whatever you have to say."

"What if he's trying to get back at you for marrying Stavros?"

"You think he's going to make me fall in love with him and then dump me?"

"I wouldn't put it past him. I know his history. He all but imploded after you left him. He lost his sports career and had to go to rehab."

I didn't want to think too long on his words. I harbored enough guilt about the past as it was, especially after hearing nearly those same things from Pierce's lips.

"I'm not responsible for another person's actions. I was eighteen at the time. I could barely handle my own choices."

"Dammit, Amelia, I'm not defending him. I just want you to know he could be finding a way to get back at you."

"Your concern is noted."

"There's something else that I'm not sure you're aware of." He shifted as if what he was about to say made him uncomfortable.

"Just say it."

"That man is into all kinds of kinky shit. He may keep it low-key, but anyone who knows him is aware of his proclivity. He likes pain, he likes control. Hell, he owns kink clubs. Are you sure you can handle it?"

My cheeks immediately heated. How many people knew about Pierce's bedroom preferences, or the clubs? A pang of jealousy prickled the back of my neck as visions of all those women I'd seen over the years on his arm flashed before me.

I pushed down the irritation and held Apollo's gaze as I said, "Who do you think it started with? We were each other's firsts."

He winced in response. "That was not what I expected to hear you say. Fuck." He rubbed his eyes. "There are some things I don't want in my head, and images of you bound, gagged, and paddled aren't one of them."

"You asked," I said, envisioning exactly what Apollo said and feeling my unsatisfied core clench.

Dammit, Pierce. I swear I'll make you pay.

"I did. To my regret, I did."

In the distance I overheard Neya's coach shouting pointers to her.

Setting my papers to the side, I leaned my arms on my

knees and rested my chin on my hands. I focused on the sparring match between Neya and one of her coaches. She moved better than I could have ever imagined doing in my youth. That girl was living the dream I'd had.

"You really can't be shocked by this. You went to that club in Paris with Stavros and me. I've never hidden my interests from you."

"I guess I always put you in the slot of the curious spectator, not a participant. I loved Stavros. God rest his soul, but the man was as vanilla as they came, despite the playboy reputation of his pre-Amelia years."

I couldn't help but smirk at the last part. Stavros had a notorious past of supposed parties, orgies, and jet-setting. All of which was a front for the ultra-private man who used the outside view of himself as a shield to keep people away.

"Should I put you in the same slot, Apollo? Spectator until the right Mistress comes along?"

His eyes widened.

"I'm well aware of what all of you are into." I gestured toward Neya.

Neya was rumored to be a well-known Mistress in Barcelona. It could explain the constant tension between her and Apollo. Maybe one day they'd act on the attraction and put the team out of their misery.

"My sex life is not the topic of discussion."

"What is it you really want to know, Apollo?"

"Are you in love with him?"

I closed my eyes for a second. "Yes. I never stopped. Now that we're together again, it's more intense than ever."

"Well, shit. What are you going to do?"

"Do about what?"

"After the fight are you coming back with us or staying?"

His question startled me. That was definitely not what I expected him to ask.

"What makes you think I'll stay? No matter how much I want it to be otherwise, my relationship with Pierce is temporary."

Now if only I could convince my heart of the same fact.

"Excluding this thing with you and Lykaios, I've never seen you as at peace as you are here. It's like you're home. Greece was never the place for you."

"I was born in Greece. I'm Greek."

"But you grew up here. You're as American as they come. When you fit somewhere, you just fit."

Apollo was right. I was home. I hadn't realized how much I had missed the US and especially Sin City until I came back.

Over the last few weeks, I'd easily reconnected with the city, the lifestyle here, and some of my old childhood friends, even making new business contacts through them.

Some had suggested I branch out and give the Lykaios

brothers a run for their money in the sporting-event arena. The idea had merit since I had just as many contacts as they did, but it would also mean uprooting Christopher.

All he'd ever known was Greece. He'd have to assimilate here as I'd had to do. Plus there was the matter of Stavros's family, who adored Christopher. Could I take him from them?

Christopher wasn't the only obstacle. My parents lived in Greece. I'd have to arrange for them to follow me. Then there was Thanos International. I truly wanted no part of it, but it was something Stavros had left in my care for Christopher.

God, I was so fucked.

"There's something else I wanted to talk to you about." Apollo's statement broke into my thoughts.

"Go ahead."

"I want to retire."

What? He was really all over the place today. He had to be kidding. MMA was his life.

I studied his face and realized he was dead serious.

"When did you make the decision?"

"I haven't made any decision. It's something I've been thinking about for a while now." He looked toward Neya. "I'm getting old, and I'd rather leave at the top of my game."

"You're that confident about beating Hugo."

He gave me the cocky grin the magazines loved to

photograph. "The boy is good. He'll probably beat my record one day, but he's not there. He knows it as much as I do."

I lifted a brow. "Then why'd you agree to this? I get the purse for this match is exorbitant, but you can live like Midas off your endorsements and past winnings for the rest of your life without ever touching the prize money from this match."

"I have my reasons. As you do for the choices you make." Apollo set his hand over mine and squeezed. "Amelia, I want you to be happy."

"I do too."

"Does Lykaios make you happy? Do you think he'll be good to Christopher?"

"Yes. On both accounts."

"Then what are you waiting for?"

"It's a lot more complicated than packing a bag."

"I know. I just want you to think it through."

"Think what through?" came a deep voice tinged with irritation.

I immediately turned toward Pierce.

⁂

P ierce

.   .   .

I couldn't hide the anger boiling up as I saw the way Apollo held Ame's hand. No one touched her that intimately but me. The media loved to say they were like siblings, but fuck that shit. He had his hands on her as if he had every right to touch her. Was this payback for leaving her wanting?

It wasn't as if she was the only one suffering. It had taken all my will to close that door on her. It was a test of both our willpower. The game I'd started with Amelia wasn't supposed to go past a few hours.

My plan had been to take her to dinner, arouse her to the point of making her crazy, and then drop her at her apartment with the order not to make herself come.

But instead of waking her with my mouth on her beautiful cunt, I'd been on the red-eye to the East Coast.

I had barely shifted my car into drive when Hagen had called telling me I had to fly to New York to put out a major fire with negotiations for a Formula One race I was trying to organize. I had no choice but to go, especially since most of the big players for the deal were going to be in the area for a conference.

I'd done my best to settle all the drama as fast as I could, but in the end, it had taken me a little over forty-eight hours to get everything calm and the deal signed.

Now here I was, looking at my woman touching another man with love and tenderness.

"Pierce. I wasn't expecting you here. I thought you were going to be in New York for the rest of the week."

The surprise and then guilt playing across Ame's face said I'd interrupted a conversation she didn't want anyone to hear.

Well, too fucking bad.

"Negotiations ended early." I held her stare and felt the energy shift between us, a second before she diverted her gaze.

She squirmed uncomfortably, giving me a small sense of satisfaction at her uneasiness.

That's right. She knew she was in trouble.

We hadn't revisited the explosion from two weeks ago or any of the lingering questions. Instead, we'd immersed ourselves into a relationship we both knew would end. The sex, the kink, the need was like nothing I'd experienced before. There was no shyness when it came to anything I wanted her to do.

If I told Amelia to drop to her knees, she would do it. If I pushed her against a wall and lifted her skirt, she'd be wet and ready for me to pound into her. If I ordered her to bend over so I could spank her, she wouldn't question it.

"Mr. Lykaios. It's good to see you." Neya came over with a smile as if she sensed the building tension.

Apollo stood, stepping over the bleachers as if he was going to protect the MMA champ from me. However,

Neya sidestepped him and offered me her hand. "Are you here to poach our talent?"

I shook her hand and returned her smile. "Just one. Your boss. I came to take her home. We have some unfinished business to address."

I heard a sharp intake of breath and almost smiled.

Apollo noticed Amelia's reaction and turned his attention to her. "Are you sure you want to leave or do you want to meet about the sponsorships?"

She glanced between Apollo and me, hesitating to answer.

Who are you going to pick, Amelia? Me or him?

After a few moments, she sighed, shaking her head. "I'll head home with Pierce."

"Are you positive?" Apollo blocked my view of Ame, making me clench my fists.

I knew there was no way I could take the behemoth of a man, but I'd try if he dared to step between Amelia and me again.

She stood, gathering her papers and stuffing them into her shoulder bag. She walked around Apollo and Neya, placing her palm on my chest. Immediately, I felt a wave of calmness that dimmed my annoyance with the fighter.

She held my gaze and responded to Apollo. "I'm sure. I need to get the penthouse ready for Christopher and my parents. They'll be here tomorrow."

The mention of Christopher made my agitation fade

further. My son would be on American soil in a little over twenty-four hours.

Amelia knew just how to get me to think straight.

Did she have any idea how she affected me?

"Enjoy your evening," Neya said, bringing my attention back to her.

She grazed her fingers over Apollo's arm. "Apollo and I will lock up the offices."

There was a tone in her words that had me recognizing a like-minded soul, and the subtle authority she was using with the giant fighter.

Well, wasn't that interesting. As was Apollo's reaction to her touch. He stared at Neya as if in a haze.

My irritation eased further.

"Ready to go?" I took the bag from Amelia and set a hand on her lower back.

We walked in silence. The only sign she felt anxiety was her shallow breaths. She licked her lips, and I had a vision of her wrapping them around my cock.

God help me if I didn't leave here without punching a hole in my pants with my rock-hard dick.

As we turned the corner leading to the staff parking lot, she spoke. "Apollo is a brother to me, nothing more."

"I didn't ask." I pushed the door open, and we were immediately hit with the bright golden light of the setting sun.

"I know what you're thinking. You're jealous of him. I wanted to make it clear where we stand."

I was going to make it super clear where we stood as soon as we were alone.

The second the doors closed behind us, Amelia grabbed me and pinned me against the brick of the building, knocking the wind out of me and causing me to drop her bag. My first reaction was to reverse our positions, but the fire and anger in her gaze kept me still.

"I let you control a lot of things when it comes to our relationship, but that is where it ends. When it come to my business or how I interact with my athletes, you have no say. I have spent the last ten years dealing with fragile male egos, I am not going to add yours to the list. Despite what I made you believe in the past, I have not now nor ever cheated. Is that clear?"

Holy shit. I liked this side of her. She was always so controlled in public, rarely letting loose outside of our private time. Well, with the exception of the club a few weeks ago.

My hands went to her waist. "Crystal."

We stared at each other. God, she was beautiful. I needed her like I needed to breathe. How the hell had I gone from wanting to destroy her to wanting to keep her forever?

As the seconds ticked by, the energy between us

shifted. Amelia's amber gaze dilated, and her breath grew shallow as her skin flushed.

I cupped her face, rubbing my thumb over her bottom lip. "Do you want to play, baby?"

"Yes."

I almost had the urge to fuck her against this building, but that was too risky, too dangerous. Plus, there was no privacy. Our security would get a very unexpected show.

"Leave your car here. We'll take mine."

A melia

Less than ten minutes later, we arrived at the residential side of the Cypress. The short ride was quiet, filled with an undercurrent of sex and desire. My underwear was soaked through and my nipples ached to the point of almost painful.

I wasn't sure what had come over me, but my temper flared and I'd lost it. Pierce acting all caveman when we were in the place where I was boss added him to the list of assholes I dealt with on a daily basis. I had to establish boundaries and make it clear that he couldn't push me around.

What surprised me was that instead of being angry at me, Pierce was turned on, like he couldn't wait to fuck me against the next available surface. I had no doubt that if privacy wasn't an issue, he would have pushed me face first against the brick of the building and had his way with me.

Pierce set his hand on my lower back as we made our way into the building. We garnered a few curious looks from passersby as they recognized us. It was hard for people to reconcile that we were lovers and the business aspect of our lives had nothing to do with the personal.

The tabloids liked to make up articles about one of us using the other for a way to rig the fight, but they were easy to ignore. The only voices that were hard to ignore were the grumblings of the Thanos board.

As predicted, Olivia was stirring things up. In less than two weeks she'd forced the company to implement policies that would change the misogynistic tendencies of selecting higher-level positions and made it a more equal playing field when it came to working with female-owned companies. Then I'd added to the board's ire with the public interest in my rekindled relationship with Pierce. The board felt that was questionable behavior and wasn't representative of the company's values. I bet they'd totally lose it if they knew the types of things Pierce and I enjoyed behind closed doors.

I looked forward to the day Olivia found a way to boot

all the assholes out. She was ruthless when it came to her mission, and she was determined to make changes.

We stepped onto the elevator, and my thoughts returned to the man by my side. He watched me with hunger.

My skin began to tingle.

He crowded me against the wall of the elevator, forcing me to tilt my head up to look at him.

"Tonight is the last time I will have access to you without restrictions. I plan to make the most of every minute."

He was right. After Christopher and my parents arrived, things between us would dramatically change. My priority would go from work and Pierce to Christopher and then everything else.

"Do you understand what I'm saying?" His fingers threaded into my hair.

I licked my now parched lips and nodded.

"I need the words. What do you understand?"

"You're going to fuck me on every surface of my apartment and I'll be lucky if I can walk tomorrow."

A wicked grin lifted his lips, making him look like the boy from so long ago. "Exactly."

The bell rang, indicating my floor. We stepped off and took the short corridor to my penthouse. I caught sight of one of my security, a petite brunette who worked for

Interpol. She lifted a brow and moved discreetly out of view.

"Since you told me about them, I've made it a game to try to spot them," Pierce said over my shoulder as I pressed my keycard against the polished metal plate of the door.

"How many have you spotted?"

"Five so far. The brunette is the one I see most often. How many are there?"

"There are twelve of them. Patricia is the one you see most often since she's on leave for the summer. She heads my security."

"She looks barely big enough to lift a child."

I shot him a glare over my shoulder. "Don't mistake size for ability. In three quick moves, she could lay you out before you even knew she'd moved."

"I believe you. Especially after I saw Penny take down Hagen when he pissed her off. She credited the training you and her coaches gave her as the reason for her abilities."

"I had to make sure she could defend herself when she traveled around the world looking for her flowers."

We stepped across the threshold of my apartment and the mood immediately changed from the easy exchange to anticipation.

"You know what to do." His whiskey-smooth voice slid over me, making goosebumps prickle my skin.

I wanted him so badly, needed him. But tonight, I needed that deeper connection.

He liked to say I grounded him when we were younger, when it was Pierce who gave me the grounding I needed to cope with the stress of the world around me.

"Pierce?" I said as he set my bag on a hallway table and moved toward me.

"Yes, Ame."

He watched me as a predator watched his prey.

"Can we put the games aside for one night? I want you to make love to me."

His face softened. "Absolutely."

He stopped a few inches from me, cupped my face and drew me toward him. The kiss was so gentle, so tender, exactly what I needed.

As he pulled back, he murmured, "For the record, every time with you is making love. Even when it's angry fucking, there's emotion there."

He lifted me into his arms as if I were a tiny, lightweight woman, instead of an anything-but-petite fighter, and carried me into my bedroom.

We kissed as we undressed each other—touching, petting, stroking every inch of skin that was bared. His touch was intoxicating, making me feel delicate and cherished.

He lowered me to the bed and settled between my legs. When he slid inside me, it felt more intimate than anything we'd shared before. It was as if our souls fused, wrapping us in a slow dance of passion and need.

Love and need overwhelmed me as my body flew over the cliff of release a second before he followed.

How was I ever going to be able to live without him again?

"Shh." Pierce wiped the dampness from my cheeks. "It's the same for me. We're going to figure this out. Now sleep, baby. Our son will be here tomorrow."

CHAPTER NINETEEN

Pierce

"Christ," I muttered, feeling the thick humidity as I walked into the Buchanan Natatorium on the campus of the University of Nevada a little after nine in the morning. I wanted to get a look at Jennifer Ellis, a prospective athlete with incredible talent but limited means. As a freshman, her times blew away records set by other female athletes in the school's swim program history. She was even close to breaking a few of mine. If I could sign her, I'd have the number-one prospect going into the next Olympic Games.

Plus, work would keep my mind off the fact I would meet my son tonight. The plan was for me to go to

Amelia's for pizza and then we'd go down to the arcade for video games.

I had never been so nervous in my life. Not even when I had my first meet at the Olympics.

"Pierce, my man."

"Carl. How's it going?" I shook hands with the head swim coach for the women's division.

"Good. I bet you're here to watch Jen practice."

"The least I can do before offering her a sponsorship."

His dark, almost black eyes gleamed. "You may have to stand in line. At this moment, she's being charmed by the competition."

I felt a twinge of annoyance. Who the fuck knew about her?

"Who?"

Carl chuckled. "A very knowledgeable nine-year-old who follows everything swim and one day plans to break your record. Those were his words, not mine."

I smiled. A kid who had goals from a young age was definitely worth meeting. I could steer him in the right direction for his training. That was, if he was serious. I'd have to talk to his parents.

I took the steps leading to the pools and came to an abrupt stop.

Jennifer was sitting with her feet in the water as she talked to a dark-haired boy with blue eyes. They laughed and splashed waves in the water.

A startled Marie Nephus stood from a set of bleachers. Amelia's mother looked between Christopher and me, unsure of what to do. I was well aware she knew Amelia and I had resumed our relationship. And I was positive she was aware of the plans for tonight. However, what I wasn't sure of was if she would try to convince Ame to return to Greece or whether she accepted my involvement in Christopher's life. Phillip, Marie's husband, touched her hand, whispering something that had her sitting back down but watching me like a hawk.

That was when Christopher spotted me. His eyes grew just as big as his grandmother's had, but his were filled with excitement instead of dread.

"It's really you." Christopher jumped up, running in my direction, and then stopped abruptly a few feet from me.

Jennifer followed close behind him.

"Mr. Lykaios. It's a pleasure to meet you. Chris here is a huge fan of yours."

"It's good to meet both of you."

I shook Jennifer's hand and then knelt in front of Christopher.

He studied me, tilting his head left and right. "I know you," he said with a thick Greek accent.

"You do? What have you heard?"

"You're Pierce Lykaios." He pulled out a figure from his pants pocket. A lump formed in my throat. "My Papa said this was you and I would have to work super hard to be like you."

I wanted to hate the man who'd taken my place but how could I when he'd spoken to my son about me?

"You want to be a swimmer?"

An offended scowl covered his face. "I *am* a swimmer."

"I'll have to see you in action sometime."

He smiled.

"Mr. Lykaios, if you would excuse me for a few minutes? I have to ask the coach a question about our meets for this week."

"Go right ahead. I'd like to get to know the boy who's going to beat my records."

"See you later, squirt." Jennifer ruffled Christopher's hair and then walked toward the locker room, leaving me with Christopher and a very agitated Marie watching over us.

"I know a secret," Christopher said. "But I'm not supposed to tell anyone but you."

"Okay, let me hear it." I lifted my ear to his lips.

He shook his head and glanced at his grandparents.

This was interesting. I offered him my hand and felt like weeping when he took it.

Would my next child with Amelia look like Christopher or his mother? Guilt hit my gut. I had all but blackmailed Amelia into the agreement. Her agreeing was the only way she'd thought to ensure my silence. I'd never have gone through with any of my threats. I'd needed some way to keep her, and at the time, coercion was the only thing that came to mind.

I'd freed Amelia from the bargain. It was her choice to stay. Plus, it was more than a bargain; we both knew it but had no clue how it would end.

I wanted her to stay, to pick me over her need to protect the Thanos name.

I pushed the thought back and focused on the boy standing before me.

"Let's go over here." I directed him to a set of benches near the locker rooms.

Once we were settled, I said, "Now, what's the secret?"

"You promise that you won't tell Mama or *Yia Yia?* Papa said it would make them sad if they knew the secret."

What the hell was he going to tell me? Thanos had been dead for two years. And what secrets could he have told a then-seven-year-old?

"Okay. I promise."

He handed me the figurine of Poseidon. "Papa told me this belonged to my dad. He said one day I'd get to meet him."

My throat went dry as a ball formed in the pit of my stomach. "What makes you think I'm your dad?"

"This belongs to you, doesn't it?"

I studied the figurine and could almost see Mama giving it to Christopher.

"Yes, it's mine."

"That means you're my dad. Aren't you? Papa would never lie to me."

Oh fuck, there was no way to answer without causing problems.

"I...it's..."

"I know you and Mama loved each other before she met Papa. I saw the magazines and newspaper articles about it. She gets sad whenever anyone talks about her life in America. Just like she gets sad when people talk about Papa. He's in heaven. Did you know?"

I swallowed and nodded my head. "I did."

"I miss him."

"It's to be expected. You loved him very much." I thumbed the cut on Poseidon's left arm.

"He would fly kites with me. Will you fly a kite with me one day?"

"I promise."

At that moment, Marie approached us, and I knew my unsupervised time with Christopher was over.

I handed Christopher the wooden carving. "It's time to go back to your grandma."

"Promise you won't tell anyone the secret?"

"I promise."

The next thing I knew, Christopher had wrapped his arms around my neck. "Thanks, Dad. I can call you that, right?"

"Um...how about when we are alone you can call me Dad but whenever anyone is around, including your mom, you can call me Pierce."

He thought for a second and then nodded his agreement.

"Bye, Pierce." Christopher grinned. "I can't wait to tell Mama we met."

I cringed inside thinking of Ame's reaction when she heard the news. I turned to grab my suit jacket from the bench and came face to face with Marie Nephus.

"*I'd like a word with you, Mr. Lykaios,*" she said in Greek.

If she was switching languages, she had something to say that she didn't want others to hear.

"*Call me Pierce.*"

"*Let me get straight to the point. Do not use Amelia to get to Christopher. She's been put through enough.*"

I glanced over to Christopher who was back to chatting with Jen while his grandfather watched over him.

"*I have no intention of hurting her.*"

Marie folded her arms across her body. "*What, exactly, are your intentions? I know she's sharing your bed. Even if she thinks she's hiding it, I know.*"

Well, fuck. How was I supposed to admit to a very conservative old lady that I was boning her daughter every chance I got?

"*I plan to marry her.*"

Surprise flashed on her face. *"Does she know this?"*

I nodded. *"She's the one who needs convincing."*

"Her life is very complicated. Things have never come easy for her even if from the outside it looked as if it had. She had to adapt to a world that wasn't meant to be hers and fill a role meant for another woman. Stavros loved her in the best way he could but not the way she needed."

"Why are you telling me this?"

"Because it has taken me less than a day to see my old Amelia returning to me. The one who all but died when she left you. I can only attribute the change to you and being back in Las Vegas."

"Was she that unhappy in her marriage?"

"No. She would never say she was. But she wasn't the Amelia I'd raised. She allowed others to mold her into who they thought she should be. And the fact she married into the Thanos dynasty and to their heir made it harder. Then when Stavros passed and she had to take on his role, it was beyond anything one person should have on her shoulders."

Was this the reason she'd wanted to continue our relationship after I'd set her free?

"What I want to know is if you love her the way she deserves? Not the girl from ten years ago but to the woman she is today."

"I never stopped loving her. What she makes me feel now is more than I ever thought possible."

My words seemed to ease the tension around her eyes.

"*Then, in that case, I give you one piece of advice. Don't give up on her. She isn't as strong as everyone believes. The reason she holds herself back is because it is all she knows.*"

"*Would you move back here if given the opportunity?*"

She smiled. "*Without thinking twice. Collin hurt our family, but I forgave him when he humbled himself for my girl.*"

Collin. The man was always there. How was I to forgive someone who all but threw me out, kept me from my dying mother, and ruined my relationship with Amelia?

"*Was it that easy to forgive him?*"

"*Yes. He took responsibility for his actions. He never once blamed anyone but himself. And we know the truth behind who forced his hand. A man like that is as much a victim as we all were.*"

At that moment, I heard Christopher call to Marie. "*Yia Yia, Pappous says it's time to go.*"

"*Coming,*" she responded before turning back to me.

"*Will you tell Ame about my meeting Christopher?*" I asked.

"*No, that is your job. After all, they are your family.*"

A melia

"I have to tell you something," were the first words I heard Pierce say when I answered my phone.

I was nervous beyond anything I'd ever experienced in my life. The only thing I could think about since I woke this morning was how Christopher was going to react to Pierce when he arrived for dinner.

"Pierce. Please tell me you're still coming?"

I saw Christopher peek his head up from his study of his Lego creation. I'd told him Pierce Lykaios was joining us for dinner when he'd gotten home from the Natatorium and he'd all but tackled me with kisses. I guess I should be happy that he hero-worshipped the athlete, so when he learned the truth of who Pierce was, he would accept it more naturally.

"Yes, I'll be there. I'm actually on my way there. I just wanted to talk to you about something before I arrive. Can you go to a room Christopher isn't in?"

Okay, that sounded ominous.

"Sure. Let me go to the office." I turned to Christopher. "Baby, Mommy needs to take this call. If you need me, I'm in the room next to your bedroom."

He nodded, half-distracted as he set his Greek-god figurines on the structure he'd created with Legos.

I took the short walkway down the hall, shutting the door before I sat in the chair behind my desk.

"Go ahead."

"Christopher knows."

The hairs on the back of my neck rose. "What do you mean he knows?"

"Exactly what I said. He knows that I'm his father. I ran into him and your parents today. He was chatting with the athlete I'm trying to recruit."

Why hadn't Mama mentioned it when I'd asked her how their first day in the US had gone? She'd smiled and said Christopher met a few of his favorite swimmers and played. Well, I guess she hadn't lied, but she hadn't told me who they were. I was going to have to discuss this with her later.

"Did you tell him?"

"No. Stavros did."

"Umm. Say that again."

"Apparently Stavros told him that I was..." Pierce released a deep breath. "His dad. That the Poseidon he carries around belonged to his dad."

"But why would he do that?" And why hadn't Stavros told me? I rubbed one of my temples.

"I don't know. Maybe he was trying to make it so the door was open to me."

"God. All these years, my baby held this secret."

"He doesn't want you to know. He made me promise

not to tell you. He said it makes you sad to remember the past."

I sighed. "It's not the past but what happened between us."

"We're changing things now."

I squeezed my eyes tight. Wanting so desperately to believe it was true.

"Why did you tell me? You could have kept it as something between Christopher and you."

"Because I don't want any secrets between us. You and Christopher are my family. I won't hurt you like that."

Family.

I swallowed as I thought about all the decisions about the future that were so uncertain.

"I'm scared I'm the one who will hurt you."

"Why don't we discuss that when we're face to face. I'm pulling up. See you in five minutes."

<hr>

The doorbell rang precisely five minutes after my call with Pierce ended. Butterflies jumped in my stomach. Why was I feeling nervous? Like I felt as a sixteen-year-old on our first date, so many years ago.

"I'll get it." Christopher ran to the penthouse entry, grabbing hold of the door handle and yanking it open. He was literally bouncing up and down when he saw Pierce.

"You came!"

"I did." Pierce stepped inside and crouched down, setting a box on the floor a second before Christopher threw himself into Pierce's arms.

A look passed over Pierce's face that had me holding in a whimper a second before he wrapped his arms around Christopher.

Pierce looked up at me, mouthing, "Thank you."

Dear God, I'd kept him from his son.

"Is that for me?" Christopher slipped from Pierce's lap and eyed the wrapped box.

"Yes, it is. Here you go." Handing him the package, Pierce stood. "Careful. It is super heavy."

Christopher swayed a bit as he held the gift. What the hell was under the paper? He shifted the box and moved to leave, but I grabbed him before he could go too far.

"Not so fast. What do you say?"

"*Efcharistó poly*...umm I mean, thank you."

Pierce gave him a smile that had my heart melting. "*Parakalo.*"

Christopher's eyes grew big and then his lips curved in an identical grin to Pierce's. "You speak Greek?"

"I do. Both my parents are Greek."

"You mean *Pappous* Collin and *Yia Yia* Rhea."

Pierce froze for a second but then nodded. "Yes."

"I like *Pappous* Collin. He buys me ice cream and tells me stories."

"Baby, why don't you go open your present and let me welcome Pierce into our home."

Christopher nodded and ran to the coffee table with the box that was almost as big as he was. Within seconds the wrapping was history, and he was squealing with excitement as he opened the box, pulling out the giant instruction manual and various bags of pieces.

It was the Lego Millennium Falcon.

"Really?" I lifted a brow as I looked into Pierce's cobalt-blue eyes.

"You're a *Star Wars* geek. I can safely assume any child of yours would be too."

"That's not what I was referring to. That set is worth eight hundred dollars."

"Let me spoil him this one time. After all, this is the first time I'm meeting him." He cupped my face, running his thumb over my lower lip. "Am I allowed to kiss you? I don't wholly know the rules."

My hand covered his on my cheek. "Neither do I."

"Then let's go with what feels right." His lips grazed mine. When he pulled back, he tucked a stray hair behind my ear. "Hi."

I laughed at how silly I felt and lifted up onto my tiptoes, giving him another quick kiss, and turned to find Christopher watching us with fascination.

After a few moments, he asked, "Are you going to marry Mama?"

He did not just ask that.

"Christopher. That's not..."

Pierce cut me off. "Yes, I am. But I may need your help to convince her."

Dear God, he did not just say that.

"Okay." Christopher nodded. "But I'll warn you. Mama is stubborn as a mule. Well, that's what *Yia Yia* says."

"I couldn't agree more," Pierce responded with a tone of humor in his voice and squeezed my waist.

My cheeks heated in mortification. These two were definitely father and son.

"Want to help me start this kit before dinner?"

My heart felt like it would explode from the joy on both their faces.

CHAPTER TWENTY

PIERCE

"This is Lykaios." I answered the phone without looking at who was calling as I pulled up to the Cypress.

I was late to dinner with Amelia and Christopher because of some last-minute meetings before the craziness of the fight took over my life.

The last month had been everything I could ever have imagined. I was getting to know my son and Amelia, and I had grown accustomed to the dynamics of our unique relationship. Rarely, if ever, would I spend the night at Amelia's, and on the occasions I had, I'd sneak out of her place before Christopher woke. I didn't want him ever to think I wanted his mother more than him.

"Pierce, son. I have to talk to you." My body stiffened, hearing Collin's voice on the line.

Why would he be calling me? I hadn't initiated any contact since I learned the truth about the past from Hagen and the only connection we had was his relationship with Amelia.

"Collin. What can I do for you?" I asked, stepping out of my car and handing the keys to the valet.

"I'm sure I'm the last person you want to hear from, but I had to call you."

I made my way into the residential lobby and toward the elevators.

Pushing the call button, I asked, "What's going on?"

"I just received word that Astros Dukas has leaked information about Christopher's paternity to the Greek press."

My blood froze.

I waited until the cab doors closed before I responded. "How would he know that I am Christopher's father?"

"Apparently, he collected hair samples from Christopher and had them run against a first cousin of Stavros. The results showed no familial relationship. He is pressing the Thanos family to call into question Stavros Thanos's last will and trust."

"The hell he is."

"I've done everything in my power to keep this from

getting out, but I've had no luck." Collin sighed. "I even called Draco for help."

"You did what? Why would you do this?"

From everything Hagen had told me, Draco would be the last person Collin would ever consider contacting. He had to have been desperate.

"Because that boy is my grandson." There was outrage in his tone. "You are my son, and Amelia is as much a daughter to me as Henna and Anaya are."

The mention of Anaya had my temper calming. Collin had proven he would do anything to protect those he cared for, even make an enemy of them.

"What do you need me to do?" I asked Collin.

"I need you to tell Amelia. She mentioned she was having dinner with you. I convinced her to leave Christopher with Marie so they could go see a new children's show premiering tonight."

"Fuck." I ran a frustrated hand through my hair. "This is all we need."

That bastard Dukas had to have planned this. He annoyed me when he'd crashed our sponsor party, and what I'd learned about him from the conversation I'd overheard Amelia having about the board made me want to take care of him the way Hagen would have back in the day, with fists and the fear of God. And I'd have no regrets whatsoever in doing it.

"Do the American outlets know?" I paced the short

space of the elevator as it ascended to Amelia's floor.

As soon as I got a chance, I would call my media manager to get staff assembled for the inevitable media shitstorm that was guaranteed to descend on us.

"I'm sure it will come out soon. The only reason I found out was because I still have friends in Greece with ties to various news agencies in Europe. They wanted to warn me about what was headed our way."

"Fuck." I punched the polished aluminum of the cab, leaving a dent.

"Exactly," Collin agreed. "I'm going to move Christopher and the Nephuses to my house. It is the most secure. You keep Amelia with you. I don't want her blindsided by the media vultures. They're ten times more aggressive here in the States than they are in Europe."

"I got it. Now my only problem is convincing her to stay put. You of all people have to know she burns the candle at both ends. And with this fight around the corner, she has more shit than usual to do. Plus, I'm going to need divine intervention to keep her from handing me my balls."

"That's what happens when you fall for a hot-blooded Greek woman. I should know."

There was a whimsy to Collin's voice that I hadn't heard before. It made me ache for a time that sometimes I believed I'd made up in my mind. I shook the thought away. I couldn't go down that rabbit hole.

"Thank you."

"You're welcome, son."

I hung up the phone, feeling a sense of urgency, dread, and hope. Urgency and dread because I was going to have to cage Amelia, and from everything I'd learned, that was how she'd lived to fit into the world of the wealthy and elite.

The hope was because this was the first conversation I'd had with Collin where I'd felt no anger toward him. It was an interaction any grown man would have with his father.

"Fuck," I muttered, stepping off the elevator.

I took a deep breath, braced myself for the conversation ahead of me, and knocked on Amelia's door.

The second it opened, I knew it was too late. There was utter devastation written all over Amelia's face. She was pale and her normally bright, shiny eyes were red-rimmed and filled with defeat.

I made my way in, taking her into my arms and holding her against me.

"I just got word from the Thanos publicist. Astros... he...I hate the bastard." She started crying. "He painted me as a whore, a gold-digger. He said this was my punishment for keeping Christopher from you."

I picked her up and carried her to the couch, cradling her body to mine. "No, baby. This is the work of a man who believes he can gain something from you."

"Oh, God." She lifted her face and covered her mouth

with her fingers. "That stupid promise Stavros made to Astros."

"What promise?"

"Right after Stavros's first wife Sara passed away, Stavros made an agreement with Astros to give his shares of Thanos International to Astros."

Why the fuck would he do that? There had to be more to this story.

"That makes no sense. Why would he do this?"

"Because Sara was the love of his life, and without her, he never planned to have children. Then after his illness, even if he changed his mind he couldn't."

She hiccupped and continued, "Then, when I married him and Christopher became his heir, Stavros assumed Astros would understand his agreement was made in grief."

"Apparently not."

Dropping her head to my chest, she sighed.

"I have spent the past ten years trying to prove everyone wrong. Do you know what it's like to be an outsider in a family like that? If it wasn't for Stavros's grandmother and a few of his cousins, I'm not sure I could have handled staying in Greece after he died."

She always seemed so strong, so in control. It pissed me off to holy hell to know she felt like she hadn't belonged.

"Do you think he was behind Stavros's death?"

She stiffened for a second, confirming my suspicion.

"I always wondered, but there was no proof. The drunk captain who hit Stavros's boat had a history of intoxicated infractions. What does it matter, anyway? It won't bring him back."

"If they prove Astros was involved, then he can be prosecuted."

"But the damage to me, Christopher, the family would be catastrophic. Things don't work the same way in Greece as they do here."

"He's dangerous."

"I know this. I've always known this. Do you really think I only have Mossad, MI6, Interpol, and CIA agents as my security detail for random visits from Draco Jackson?"

Wait a second. She said Draco.

"What?" I couldn't hold back the roar in my voice. "You met with a mobster and didn't think I should know?"

She grimaced. "He's not so bad. He's kind of sweet."

"Amelia. Draco Jackson is not sweet. He is a cold-hearted bastard who fucked up my family."

"I'm not condoning his actions. I was just trying to—"

I cut her off. "We're going to discuss Draco at a later date. Right now, we need to figure out what to do about Astros."

"There is nothing to figure out." She cocked a hand on her hip. "I know how to handle it."

That was when I noticed the carry-on luggage in the hallway.

"Where are you going?"

"To Greece."

My heart dropped.

"What do you mean? You can't just up and leave a week before the fight. You're going to miss the weigh-in."

She ignored me and said, "I already had my luggage sent to the plane. We're scheduled to leave around seven tonight. I arranged it so Mama and Papa will watch Christopher during the day and at night he'll stay with you. It'll give you a chance to get to know each other without me around. For you to see what it's like to parent an almost-ten-year-old when it's not all fun and games."

I listened to her ramble. She couldn't be serious.

"So let me get this right—you're planning to combat the tabloids by going to Greece, where the media will swarm you like vultures?"

"I have no choice. I need to face *Yia Yia* Syl. I need to do damage control for Thanos International."

"Who's Syl?" She couldn't be referring to Sylvia Thanos.

"Stavros's grandmother. She has always been good to me and deserves an explanation. She loves Christopher more than you can imagine. I know it's probably breaking her heart hearing all this. Stavros never wanted her to know."

Amelia had to know that the matriarch of the Thanos empire had a reputation for pure ruthlessness and cunning. From the research Adrian Kipos had given me, Sylvia liked to project a gentle nature, making the world believe she was a sweet lady who only wanted to cook and play with her great-grandchildren.

But in fact, Sylvia was probably more dangerous than Draco. She'd become a widow at the age of thirty with two young children. Instead of mourning, she'd taken over her husband's shipping empire in a world run by men. She'd used the same tactics as her male counterparts for contracts, which included some questionable dealings, to triple the size of her family's fortune in ten years.

And by the time she'd retired and handed her company to her sons, she'd amassed a corporation valued in the billions. There was nothing fragile or delicate about Sylvia Thanos.

The fact Amelia seemed to have no clue this woman she respected had a reputation scarier than Draco's boggled the mind.

Fuck. The determination on Amelia's face told me she wasn't going to listen to reason.

"What about us?"

"What do you mean, what about us?"

"Exactly what I said. You and me. Where do we stand?"

"We're a couple and parents to Christopher."

"I want more."

She closed her eyes, causing a tear to fall. "Pierce, everything is so fucked up."

"No, it's pretty simple. I want you, me, and Christopher to be a family. It doesn't matter if you do or don't get pregnant again. I knew that first night I saw you at the gym when I was seventeen and you were barely sixteen, that I'd found the one person who was meant to be mine. It hasn't changed."

Her phone beeped.

"I have to go." She stood, wiping her face with the back of her hand, and grabbed her carry-ons. "I promise we'll talk about the future when I get back," she said as she approached me, lifted up on tiptoes to kiss my lips, then moved to the door.

"You don't have to go. We can handle this from here."

"I don't have a choice. I have to save some semblance of Stavros's legacy. He deserved so much more than this scandal. He was a good man. He gave me a life after my world fell apart."

Her words were like a knife to the gut. I was always going to compete against a dead man.

"Will you ever love me the way you loved Thanos, or am I kidding myself?"

She froze at my question, her fingers flexing on the door. "That's the thing. I never loved Stavros the way I loved you. The way I love you. You stole a part of my heart and I never got it back. Now I'm asking you to watch out for our son and wait for me."

* * *

Amelia

My hands shook as my helicopter approached the giant mansion that belonged to my grandmother-in-law. This property should have looked gaudy with its gargantuan size and Parthenon-styled pillars. But it fit with the island it sat atop as if it were designed with the cliffs and environment in mind. It also fit the larger-than-life woman who resided in the place.

How was she going to react when she saw me? Would she hate me for marrying Stavros with another man's child in my belly? Would she shun Christopher?

My boy adored his *progiagiá*. There wasn't a time when he didn't smile when he thought of her.

I had to be sensible. How would I react if I learned in the tabloids that the boy I viewed as my great-grandson wasn't in fact mine or any real relation?

I waited for the all-clear and stepped out of the copter. The wind from the propellers blew my hair out of its braid, and I knew there was no hope of taming it. I should have remembered to wear a scarf.

An attendant approached me, gesturing to follow him.

We took the path leading to the house and entered through a side door. The second I stepped across the threshold, the rich scent of spices reached my nose.

Sylvia was in the kitchen. No matter who the guest, she'd organize a feast not only for the taste buds but also for the senses.

"Cara, I'm so happy you're here," said a cheery voice in Greek, a few seconds before a beautiful silver-haired woman dressed in a designer outfit covered by a large apron came out of a corner door.

Sylvia engulfed me in a tight hug, kissing both my cheeks and pulling back long enough to study my face.

"Yia Yia, *how are you?"*

"Better than you." She rubbed the dark circles under my eyes and *tsked. "Come. I want you to eat, and then you can clear up all the nonsense I've been hearing."*

I cringed.

The matriarch of the Thanos empire was stronger and had more life than any other ninety-year-old woman I'd ever known. Hell, she had more energy than women half her age. But she also was a force one should be wary of when riled.

"I'm not sure where to begin." It was the truth.

She guided me toward the kitchen. *"At the beginning."* She paused. *"You didn't bring Christopher?"*

Shaking my head, I said, *"He stayed in the US with my parents and..."* I paused, taking a deep breath, *"...and Pierce."*

"Good. He doesn't need to be here. But I want to see him before school starts. Now let's eat."

We spent the next few minutes filling our plates and settling on the terrace overlooking the Mediterranean Sea. For a woman who'd never known a life without exorbitant amounts of money at her disposal and servants to do her bidding, she was one of the most down-to-earth people I knew. She would rather do things herself than have people wait on her day and night.

Maybe that was why I adored her so much. She knew I hadn't come from money or affluence but had treated me as her equal from the second Stavros introduced us.

We began to eat as we'd done countless times over the years, but instead of the comfortable silence we usually shared, I was anxious and just wanted to get the fallout over with.

Setting my fork on my plate, I said, *"I'm sorry."*

"What are you apologizing for?" She tilted her head, studying me. *"I should be the one begging for forgiveness. I allowed that horrible Astros to stay in our lives. I knew he only befriended Stavros for his money and connections. It only proves my belief that he would expose Christopher's*

paternity in the tabloids. Trash is what he is. Good thing my friend Draco is going to take care of him."

I stared at her as if she'd lost her mind. I couldn't have heard her correctly. Did she know about Christopher? Wait a second, had she just said *Draco?*

"I'm not sure if I understand what's going on. You know Draco Jackson?" I picked up a glass of water, bringing it to my lips for a sip.

"Yes. Just as I know Collin Lykaios. He courted Tania, my sister's eldest daughter, before he married Rhea. If Tania hadn't run away with the gardener, I'm positive Collin would have married her. But then again, he wouldn't have met Rhea and then we wouldn't have my Christopher." She waved her hand. *"That's a story for another day. Where was I?"*

"Draco."

I swore it was through her that Christopher got his short attention span and nonstop stream-of-consciousness talking. They may not share blood but all the time they spent together must have rubbed off on him.

"Ah, yes. I've known Draco for the last ten years. I didn't like him in the beginning. He thought to hurt you and Stavros by telling me you carried another man's child. When he realized I was as mean as Draco thought he could be, especially when it came to my family, he decided it was better for us to be friends than adversaries. Now he helps me

keep an eye on some of my interests in exchange for my influence in keeping the authorities from his door."

I was really having a hard time understanding what I was hearing. I searched the table and spotted the wine. I poured myself a large glass full and drank every drop down without thinking twice.

As the alcohol began to calm my mind, I asked, *"Yia Yia, are you telling me that you knew Stavros wasn't Christopher's father?"*

"Stavros was his father! My boy loved Christopher from the moment the doctor placed him in his arms." She slammed her fist on the table, making me jump.

"You're right." I set my hand over hers. *"He was and will always be Christopher's Papa."*

"Now stay quiet, so I can tell you my story."

I kept my mouth shut and nodded my agreement.

"I knew Stavros was sterile. Who do you think paid for his care in Thailand and kept his illness a secret? My money and power bought the silence of all who came in contact with him."

Holy shit. Who was this woman? And what had she done with the sweet *Yia Yia* I'd known for the last decade? It was like she was a mob queen in the guise of an internationally successful businesswoman and timid Thanos matriarch.

"Don't look at me like that. You think only mobsters can

be ruthless. I will slit a man's throat without thinking twice if he threatens anyone I love.

"Now back to what I was saying. When Stavros met and married you, I knew Draco had forced Collin Lykaios to orchestrate the demise of your relationship with his son. Collin would do anything to protect his family, even become the enemy if it meant they were safe. He is truly a better man than the world believes. I'm so happy you forgave him." She patted my hand. "He deserves some happiness. First, his wife betrays him, and then he has to pay for protecting the child she had with the ones who were his."

Dear God. I had to be in a parallel universe.

"How do you know all this?" I couldn't help but ask.

"Collin and I stayed in touch over the years. In fact, I was the one to give him the money to move to America and start his casinos. Just because Tania was an idiot didn't mean I was. I saw potential in the boy. He'd come from nothing and made something of himself."

"What does any of this have to do with Stavros and me?"

"Collin and I arranged for you to meet Stavros. Well, actually I was the one who gave him the push. He was coming up on the anniversary of Sara's passing, and I wanted to distract him, so I arranged for tickets to your taekwondo fight. He was a big fan of anything martial arts, and since the games were in Europe that year, he was more *than happy to go. The events that occurred afterward transpired better than whatever I could have planned."*

I couldn't help but sound defensive when I said, *"Nothing happened between us at the Olympics. It wasn't until a month later that we met again and we eloped."*

"I know this. You aren't the type of woman to sleep with two men. Though your relationship with Collin's son wasn't one I would approve of a teenager engaging in." She gave me a disapproving shake of her head.

Oh hell. Someone kill me now. She knew what Pierce and I were into and I wasn't going to ask what source told her. She apparently was very resourceful, in ways I could never have imagined.

"Yia Yia, where do we go from here? Because of me, the press is questioning Christopher's and my place in the Thanos family."

"Who cares what anyone thinks? You two belong to me, and I dare anyone to say otherwise. Especially that weasel Astros. I should have gotten rid of him years ago when he first started sniffing around Stavros. That idiot probably thought I'd honor that stupid agreement he made with Stavros after he lost Sara and my newborn diséngonos. The bastard took advantage of a grieving man. He's a coward." She clenched her jaw and raised her fist. *"If I ever see him again, I will gut him with my own hands."*

"Please don't get worked up. Remember your blood

pressure." I tried to soothe her, but I knew it was a moot point.

"*Stop coddling me. Now tell me, are you going to address the press or not?*"

"*What am I supposed to say?*"

"*That your boy is lucky enough to have two fathers who love him. One who is watching over him from heaven and another who will be the type of father every boy wishes he had. You can also add in that Lykaios loves you.*"

My lips trembled at her words. "*He does love me.*"

"*Does he know you love him?*"

I looked away, staring at the sky blue water and said, "*No. Umm. Yes. It's just that I don't think he believes me.*"

"*Then you need to convince him. Stop trying to fit into this mold you've created in your head of what the perfect Thanos wife is supposed to resemble. You were always perfect the way you were. If only the other granddaughters-in-law were half of what you are, I'd be more inclined to invite them here.*"

My heart swelled. I so loved this woman. She knew exactly my insecurities and what to say to assuage them.

"*I want you happy, Amelia. You gave my Stavros some of the happiest years of his life. The least I could want is the same for you. Don't lose your second chance. I've investigated Collin's boy. He's a bit hot-tempered, but he's a good man. And not bad to look at, if I do say so myself.*"

I laughed. I couldn't help it.

"*I love you, Yia Yia.*"

"*Of course you do. Now promise this one thing.*"

I waited for her to continue.

"*Once you marry Collin's son, you will visit me at least twice a year from America. And your wedding better be here on the island.*"

"*Anything you ask, Yia Yia.*"

CHAPTER TWENTY-ONE

Amelia

"Ms. Thanos, your car is outside on the tarmac and will take you to Mr. Lykaios's home as instructed," said a man in a three-piece suit as he guided me to the waiting car mere steps from Sylvia's private jet.

"Thank you," I said as I waited for the jet doors to open.

Immediately, I was hit by the unbearable, dry Vegas heat, and a sheen of sweat formed on my brow.

God, it was only nine in the morning and it had to be over a hundred and ten today.

Quickly as possible, I rushed down the steps and slipped into the waiting SUV, releasing a deep sigh and dropping my head back onto the headrest.

It had been a whirlwind five days.

I spent my days handling business related to Thanos International and Thanos Sports and my nights with Sylvia, planning for the future and learning about the woman behind the empire.

I was still in a bit of a haze from all that I'd discovered, about Sylvia herself and the history of the man who held my heart. It was something I'd have to discuss with Pierce.

There could be no secrets between us if there was any hope of making our relationship work.

When I'd called to check up on Christopher, both Mama and Pierce insisted they had everything under control Stateside, Christopher-wise, and fight-wise, and that my focus should be settling things in Greece. Even when I touched base with Penny and Henna, they closed ranks, giving me only enough information to keep me from worrying.

Thank goodness for Emery. His updates via phone, email, and text kept me from going crazy with all the unknowns about Apollo and my other fighters. He'd also helped ease the guilt I felt for missing the weigh-in. According to him, the news outlets had tried to make the friendly rivalry between Apollo and Hugo into a war-of-the-continents thing. Neither fighter had corrected the assumption, since it meant more media coverage and viewers.

At least the American media was staying focused on the fight for the most part, instead of my personal life.

The European press hounded me nonstop as soon as they learned of my arrival, but thanks to my security as well as the extra personnel Sylvia and Pierce had arranged, no one could get within ten feet of me without approval.

At times I thought it was overkill, but it was better than being swarmed by the media. Whenever someone got within shouting distance of me, they'd ask questions I wasn't ready to answer and insist they had a right to know. The press wasn't anywhere as invasive as they were in America, and it made me wonder what Pierce was dealing with.

He could handle anything. I'd missed him more than I'd expected. And even more so after I'd accepted my plans for the future.

Pierce made me feel safe, loved, *owned.*

The last part had my body tingling. A surprise yawn escaped my lips followed by my stomach growling.

God, I was sleepy, hungry, and horny.

We still had a good thirty minutes before arriving at the hotel. A little power nap was in order, especially since I couldn't do anything about my latter two problems.

I tucked my sweater around me and closed my eyes as I drifted off to sleep.

Pierce

I paced as I waited for Amelia to arrive. This week had felt like the longest of my life. Yes, I was thankful to have one-on-one time with Christopher. It had given me an opportunity to get to know the little boy who I learned was more like me than I could ever imagine. He had no fear and when riled had a temper that could have rivaled mine as a child. I knew I'd surprised him when I reprimanded him for his temper tantrum after Marie had come to take him home one evening.

That day, Christopher's view on what a dad's role was changed. He knew he could have fun with me, but I'd tell him off when it was warranted.

I never imagined how overwhelming and amazing it would feel to be a father. It gave me perspective of how devastating it must have been for Collin to hurt Hagen, Zack, and me in order to protect us.

My interaction with Christopher and his pure love for Collin had also pushed me to call him and see if he wanted to meet. Instead of accepting as I expected, he'd declined, worrying that if we met, it would cause problems for me with Zack. But I'd felt the emotion and longing to connect.

God, I was literally living through a Greek drama.

I pushed a hand through my hair.

The doorbell rang, making my pulse jump, and all thoughts disappeared but those of the woman on the other side of the door. I wanted her, needed her more than ever before in my existence.

The second I opened the door, I grabbed her, pushing her against the nearest wall.

"Well hello to you too." Her breath came out a hard gasp.

"Answer one question. Do you want to talk or fuck?"

The flush on her skin and her dilated caramel gaze told me the answer, but I waited for her response.

"Fuck. I want to fuck."

"Excellent." My fingers fisted into her hair as my mouth covered hers.

She tasted of the sweet-and-sour candy she liked to eat by the bagful.

Her tongue pushed past my lips, deepening the kiss and igniting the need burning in my blood into a raging fire. Cupping her ass, I lifted her against my throbbing cock and carried her to the dinner table, setting her on the edge.

"What are you doing?" she asked between kisses.

Her fingers gripped the T-shirt I'd thrown on when I'd gotten the call she was coming to the penthouse.

"What does it look like? I'm going to have my breakfast."

She touched my face. "Okay."

I set a hand on her throat, sliding it down to her

beautiful hard-peaked breasts and lower until I reached the hem of her blouse. I lifted it over her head and threw it behind me. Next went her bra, followed by her pants and underwear. When she was gloriously naked, I took two cloth napkins and tied her ankles to the legs of the table, giving me an unfettered view of her needy pussy.

Slowly, I pushed her back onto the table and then proceeded to lick, suck, and worship every inch of her soft skin, purposely avoiding the one spot where she wanted my touch. By the time I was done, she was writhing with need, legs straining against the ties, pussy weeping for attention.

"Do you want more?"

"Yes. Please, Pierce. I want to come. It's been seven days. P-p-please," she moaned, tossing her head side to side and gripping my shoulders.

"How do you want to come, baby? With my mouth, my fingers, or my cock?" I blew on her slick, swollen cunt, making her shiver.

Fuck. I could smell her desire. It was a heady mix that had my head spinning and body raging to bury myself balls-deep in her dripping heat.

She arched up, breasts heaving. "Yes, yes, yes."

I sucked one nipple into my mouth, biting the berry-shaped tip. "Yes to what, baby?"

"Anything, everything. I don't care, just do something,"

she demanded as her fingers twined in my hair, gripping it in a hard, commanding hold.

I captured her hands and pinned them to the table. "Hold the edge and don't let go."

Her fingers dug into the polished wood, and I had no doubt she had permanently marked the expensive furniture.

I slid down her body, dropping to my knees. I stared at the delicious juices coating her sex and licked my lips. Leaning forward, I took a long deep swipe, from back to front.

Immediately her back bowed and a whimper escaped her lips. I repeated the motion two more times before I dived into her delicious cunt. I gorged on the taste of her, pressing deep into her quickening channel in a rhythm I knew would drive her insane and push her to the release she craved. A second before her orgasm exploded out of her, I pinched her clitoral nub, giving her the extra surge of pleasure-pain that would heighten her release.

"Pierce. Oh, Pierce."

As she began to come down, I dropped my lounge pants and positioned my cock at her still-spasming entrance. I hissed as I pushed inside her, stretching her with shallow thrusts until my girth worked its way inside the swollen, pulsing tissue of her sex.

She lifted her hips to meet my movement, grinding down on me, trying to suck my dick back into her.

"Fuck me harder, Pierce."

Her demand caused something to snap in me, releasing all the pent-up need I had for this gorgeous woman. I gripped her thighs, tugging her partway off the table, and began to pound. I fucked her like a madman, loving the feel of the way her muscles gripped and relaxed with each thrust. Never was there a woman more perfect for me, and I'd be dammed sure she knew she was mine.

"I'm never letting you go," I said between thrusts.

"Why are you talking? Just fuck me."

I stopped moving, and she cried out, "Nooo."

"If you don't want me to stop, then pay attention."

I sank back into her liquid heat.

"You're mine, Amelia. Time and distance haven't changed it. But this time—"

I pulled out and slammed back in, making her gasp.

"—I will chase you around the world."

Thrust.

"And I won't ever let you go."

Thrust.

"You belong to me."

Thrust, thrust.

I clenched my teeth, trying to hold in my orgasm. Neither of us was going to come unless she accepted how I felt.

"Do you understand?"

"Yes," she screamed. "I'm yours. I've always been yours."

At her admission, I worked my fingers between us and strummed her clit until her orgasm imploded and spurred mine. I began to shoot deep in her, calling her name and knowing this woman owned my heart.

As my heart calmed, I untied her and carried her limp body to my bedroom. After cleaning her, I crawled in behind her, drawing her to my body.

"So are you staying, or is this going to become a long-distance thing?"

I meant what I'd said. I'd chase her across the world, but we weren't going to end. Then one day she was going to marry me, another child or not.

I waited for her answer, and then heard the heavy sound of her breathing and realized she was sound asleep.

CHAPTER TWENTY-TWO

Amelia

Twelve hours after the mind-blowing sex in Pierce's penthouse, I entered the holding area where Apollo and our team waited for the cue announcing the athlete procession. There wasn't an empty seat, and the pay-per-view revenue was going to set a historic record. It boggled my mind to think about how much money was exchanging hands today. The world's eyes were on Vegas, specifically the center ring in Lykaios Arena.

So far the winners and losers were evenly matched. Pierce's fighters had taken half of the lower-level fights and mine had the other half, with a sprinkling of winners from other organizations. The one cherry for me was that Neya had all but made dust of her opponent. Her win was unanimous across the judges, and there was a buzz about coordinating a fight where women were the main attraction of the night.

I knew it would be a long time before a women-only fight could bring in the dollars the men brought, but this was a step in the right direction.

"I'm glad you could make it to the fight," Apollo said as I walked up to him. "For a woman who likes to be early, you were cutting it close."

Apollo sat on a bench, clenching and unclenching his taped hands. He was nervous, despite the confidence he liked the world to see. There wasn't a fight he'd entered where he didn't have the same reaction.

I leaned down and kissed his forehead. "You know me. I have to make a fashionable entrance."

I greeted Emery and the rest of the training staff and then turned my attention back to Apollo.

When our gazes caught, he gestured toward the women's locker room. "How is she?"

"Flying high. A few of the kicks will leave healthy-sized bruises, but nothing a long vacation won't do wonders for. Maybe you can join her. You could use a little R&R."

"I'll be a washed-up retired fighter after this, so you never know."

"You still confident about your decision?" I asked,

wanting to make sure he was absolutely sure about the announcement he was going to make after the fight.

"Are you positive about *your* decision?" Apollo countered.

I smiled. "Without a doubt. I have to stop trying to fit into a mold meant for another woman and...forgive myself for the decisions I made as a scared teen."

"It's about time."

"I couldn't agree more." I gave him a smile.

"So I take it your visit with Sylvia was productive."

"More than you could imagine. Under that sweet-old-lady demeanor, she's a woman who won't think twice about shanking anyone who hurts her family."

Apollo snorted. "You just figured this out? She's as scary as she is loving."

"She misses you. She said it enough times. I'd make sure to visit as soon as you get back home."

"It's one of the first things on my agenda. Plus no sane man would give up a chance to eat her amazing food."

"Especially one who's had to watch his diet like a hawk for the last few months."

The music started, and I heard the entrance music for Hugo, which made me think of Pierce.

I'd slipped from bed before he'd woken, and I knew he'd wanted to talk. I hadn't been ready. Before we had the conversation that was imperative, I had to make sure everything was in order for the plan to work.

"Time to go, champ." Emery clasped Apollo on the back.

As he stood, I wrapped my arms around his waist. "Stay focused. Nothing is a sure thing. And don't, let me repeat, *don't* get hurt. You're too important to me."

Releasing him, I felt a hum of anticipation fill me, a mixture of butterflies and excitement. It was almost like what I'd experienced during that Olympic match so many years ago. I'd gone in thinking I was an underdog and came out a gold medalist.

"Ready to go see our boy make toast of Hugo?" Neya came up behind me. "Security has our seats waiting."

"By all means, let's go."

The roar as we moved through the arena was deafening. Cameras, lights, and music overwhelmed the senses. I stood in front of my seat and searched the crowd for Pierce. He was positioned across the ring with Hagen, Penny, and Zack near him. Penny was tucked against Hagen's side with a proprietary hand gripping her waist.

Then I noticed Draco. He was surrounded by three of his grandsons. To their right was a stern yet handsome man who had a Hagen-like hold on Lana. She waved to me, blowing kisses and jumping up and down. Pierce noticed the interaction between us and shook his head. There was a lift of his brow when his attention stayed on me, and I shrugged.

I guessed I was going to have to tell him I was Lana's

friend and that in the future we'd be flying to Bora Bora for a wedding.

"How are you, *kopella mou*?" I heard Collin say as he took his seat next to me. "I heard you've had a few interesting days. Took a trip to Greece, did you?"

His eyes twinkled with happiness as he smiled at me but then dimmed a bit as he looked across to his sons.

"I did." I tucked my arm into his. "I wanted to say this now, and I won't mention it again."

"Go on." There was a tone of concern in his voice.

"It's nothing like that. I just wanted to say thank you."

"For what?"

"All that you sacrificed for your children and those who weren't. You deserve so much."

His eyes filled, but he kept looking toward the main stage. "Sylvia talks too much."

"Only when she has something to say. Just know, it's okay to forgive yourself. I've learned this."

He lifted my hand, kissing my knuckles. "I will consider it, once my boys understand, especially Zacharias."

It may be a long time for that. I knew the wounds were buried deep in each of the men, especially Zack.

"Well, in the meantime, you have a grandson who adores his *Pappous* Collin. He wants you to take him for ice cream and tell him funny stories."

A watery smile touched his lips. "Then that's what I'll do."

At that moment, the announcer began to read the rules, and the crowd grew louder in preparation for the fight.

P ierce

"Y ou did exceptionally." I patted Hugo's shoulder as we made our way into the locker room. "Next time you'll have him."

He blew out a breath, wiping the sweat dripping down his face. "From your mouth to God's ears."

My heart ached for the kid. He had given it his all, but it was a longshot for him to win. Apollo had too many years and wins under his belt to make some of the mistakes Hugo unexpectedly made. He was young, and I knew with some intensive training, he'd be ready when he had his next match.

"Go freshen up and we'll hit the press circuit together."

"So how does it feel to lose to your woman?" Hugo asked, watching me with sharp eyes.

"Not as bad as I thought it would. Though I'm sure I'll hear about it for a while to come."

The fact she would gloat wouldn't bother me in the least. All that mattered was that she was mine.

I was still going to paddle her ass for disappearing before we could have any discussion about the future or what had fully transpired while she was in Greece. And neither of us had addressed the issue of the press that hounded us or the constant inquiries for comment on the paternity of Christopher. If I had a choice, I would shout it from the rooftops, but this was Amelia's decision.

We should have had breakfast and talked when she arrived. Instead I jumped her. Then again, I'd spent nearly every night inside her for weeks, and going days without the touch, taste, or feel of her body had been torture.

God, the woman made me crazy. Crazy for wanting her, crazy in love with her.

It took Hugo thirty minutes to clean up and give a few small one-on-one interviews before we made it up to the main media stage.

The second Hugo climbed the steps, Apollo approached, shaking his hand and pulling him into a bear hug. From the smiles on both their faces, there were no hard feelings after the beat-down poor Hugo had taken. My guess was that Apollo was going to take the young fighter under his wing.

I remained a little off the stage, as did Amelia, letting

the fighters and coaches go through a play-by-play and Q and A with the reporters.

As the session was wrapping up, a reporter stood and asked, "Apollo. We need you to clarify a rumor. Was this your last match? Are you officially retiring?"

He remained quiet for a few moments, before speaking. "Yes. As of today, I will no longer fight professionally. I feel it is an honor to be part of such a prestigious community, but it is time for me to pursue other ventures. Plus, I believe my body has taken enough abuse." He rubbed a bruise forming on his jaw and mock-glared at Hugo, causing the audience to laugh.

"Apollo, one more question. Now that you've announced your retirement, what are your plans? Are you leaving the sporting world altogether?"

He glanced over at Amelia, and I felt as if they were sharing some special communication.

After she nodded, he answered.

"No. I'm actually going to still be in the thick of things, but on the opposite side. You are now looking at the Chief Operating Officer of the European division of Thanos Sports."

I stiffened, and the crowd erupted in a plethora of questions. I couldn't have heard him right. I shifted and saw Amelia watching me.

The intensity of her gaze made my heartbeat

accelerate. Was she staying? Was she giving me what I wanted more than anything?

Once the noise lowered, another reporter asked, "Would this have to do with the reports that Amelia Thanos's son is, in fact, Pierce Lykaios's?"

Oh fuck. This was not the time or place.

"We're here to discuss the sports world, not tabloid fodder." Apollo glared at the man who posed the question.

I moved to end the press conference, but Amelia walked up next to Apollo, setting a hand on his back. They spoke in hushed tones and Apollo sighed, stepping to the side.

"I'll answer the question. Actually, I'll make a statement and then I will never respond to questions on this subject again." There was an authority in her voice I'd never seen her use and made me realize this was how she'd made her company into a powerhouse.

"As a teenager, I had a relationship with a young swimmer, Pierce Lykaios. We fell in love and were together for two years. Through circumstances that I won't go into, we broke up. I kept the fact I was pregnant from him." She turned her attention to me as another murmur went through the crowd.

She was letting the world know the truth. She loved me. Anyone who looked at her would see it in her eyes. I swallowed, trying to push away the emotions locked in my throat, and forced myself to stay where I stood.

"Shortly after I left Pierce, I met a wonderful man who I married. He loved my child as if he were his own. However, he passed away in a tragic accident. A few months ago, Pierce and I rekindled our romance with him knowing he fathered a child with me. We planned to keep the news a secret until the time was right for our son, but others took that choice from us.

"Now we are here today focusing our energy on a personal family issue instead of these remarkable athletes sitting before us. And for the record, Pierce Lykaios is my family."

Her words had all the blood rushing to my head.

"The next time anyone asks me a non-business-related question," she continued, "you will be ignored. The sporting world is no place for tabloid drama."

She stepped away from the microphone and moved off the stage, coming toward me.

She stopped a few feet from me, a blush warming her cheeks. "How did I do?"

"You're pretty formidable when riled," I managed to say after I got my throat to cooperate.

"I guess some of *Yia Yia* Syl's traits rubbed off on me."

The flashes of the cameras brought both of us out of our stupor.

"Let's go somewhere private."

She nodded, and I led her toward a hallway that opened into an area filled with arena offices. After punching in the code, we entered the bright and aesthetically pleasing area.

It hit me then. Collin hadn't change the code. It was his wedding date.

I could still remember running through this building as a child when there was sawdust everywhere and the happy laughter of Mama and Collin's banter as they discussed colors that made a pleasing work environment.

I pushed the memories back and focused on the beautiful woman before me.

"So what happens next?" I asked, leaning against the closed door, folding my arms.

She set a hand next to my head and the other on my chest, moving forward until her mouth was a hairsbreadth from me. "I assumed it was obvious."

I resisted the need to touch her. Her scent was intoxicating, something I couldn't stop craving.

"Spell it out for me, so there's no confusion."

"I want you." She nipped my bottom lip. "Mind, body, and soul."

"And?" My voice was thicker than I wanted it to be. This woman had me twisted in ways no other had ever done to me.

She bit down hard this time on my lip, licking the place where her teeth had grazed, and making my cock jump in response. "And I'm going to keep you."

"Tell me what that means." I gripped her waist. I couldn't help myself.

"It means I want us to be a family. Like the one you imagined having. You, Christopher, and me. We're not going back to Greece."

Hope bloomed. This was really happening.

"And your businesses?" I threaded my fingers into her hair, tugging her head back, and stared into her caramel-hued eyes.

She smiled up at me. "Well, you see, I signed over my role as Chairman of Thanos International to Lucas and Olivia Thanos. They were born for managing the empire. They'll only call on me if I need to make critical decisions."

"And what about your promotion company? It's your baby."

"I'm not sure if you heard the news, but I just hired a well-known martial artist to take over my European interests. This will allow me to expand my empire to North and South America. I believe my future husband needs some healthy competition. It's not fair for him to dominate the market."

I swallowed. "You're getting married?"

"Yes. There is this former Olympian I've got my heart set on. He told me that he would own me, feed my need to submit, and fuck me hard."

"Does he do all of those things?"

"Absolutely. Plus, he does this one other thing."

"What's that?"

"He loves me."

I drew her to me and said, "Yes he does. He will love you until his dying breath."

The End

Master of Revenge
God of Vegas, Book 3

www.books2read.com/masterofrevenge

We are rivals. Sworn enemies. And he is the only man to ignite a fire in my soul.

I walk a fine line between control and chaos, defined by my past and driven by my future. Nothing can stop me from protecting those I love.

Zack Lykaios is cunning and dangerous. He wants to destroy everything I've built on his ruthless march to the top.

All that I am, or ever will be, says I should avoid him.

Still, I've been tempted. One card game. One night of all-consuming passion. One craving I can't deny. One need I can never quench.

Wanting him can only lead to disaster. Loving him is guaranteed to destroy my world.

Read the first book in the Gods of Vegas Series:

www.books2read.com/masterofsin

It was always him...

The one I shouldn't want, shouldn't crave, the one who could destroy my carefully built life.

Hagen Lykaios was the essence of sin, indulgence, and danger - everything I knew to avoid.

All it took was one unexpected touch, and he consumed me, left me begging, needy, and hungry for more.

He said if I entered his world he would corrupt me, own me, and change all that I had ever known...and you know what? **_I went anyway._**

ABOUT THE AUTHOR

Inspired by her years working in corporate America, Sienna loves to serve up stories woven around confident and successful women who know what they want and how to get it, both in – and out – of the bedroom.

Her heroines are fresh, well-educated, and often find love and romance through atypical circumstances. Sienna treats her readers to enticing slices of hot romance infused with empowerment and indulgent satisfaction.

Sienna loves the life of travel and adventure. She plans to visit even the farthest corners of the world and delight in experiencing the variety of cultures along the way. When she isn't writing or traveling, Sienna is working on her "happily ever after" with her husband and children.

Sign up for her newsletter to be notified of releases, book sales, events and so much more.
www.SiennaSnow.com
authorsiennasnow@gmail.com

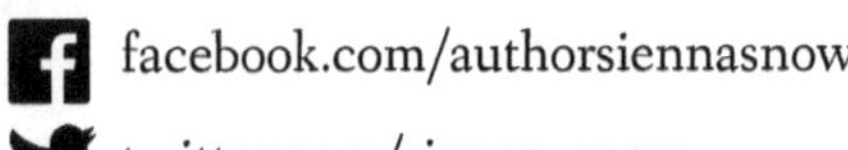 facebook.com/authorsiennasnow

twitter.com/sienna_snow

instagram.com/bysiennasnow

BOOKS BY SIENNA SNOW

Rules of Engagement

Rule Breaker

Rule Master

Rule Changer

Politics of Love

Celebrity

Senator

Commander

Gods of Vegas

Master of Sin

Master of Games

Master of Revenge

Master of Secrets

Master of Control

Collections

Take Me To Bed: Bedime Quickies

Intrigued By Love

Reckless Romeo (A Cocky Hero Club Novel)

Kings of Cyprus

Coming Fall 2020

www.ingramcontent.com/pod-product-compliance
Lightning Source LLC
Chambersburg PA
CBHW051639180726
48284CB00006B/1789